★

Rashida knocked on the door of the master bedroom. Again the only response was silence.

Rashida looked at Martha. Martha sighed and nodded again. Rashida turned the knob and opened the door.

And Martha found that even to an aged female civilian, it can happen twice.

Arnold Stern was dead. Martha and Rashida found him—what was left of him—behind the closed door to the master bedroom. He was lying between the bed and the chest of drawers, his ruined face caked with brown dry blood. The room, in spite of the wide-open windows, smelled ever so faintly of rotten meat.

★

"Highly recommended."

— *Library Journal*

Previously published Worldwide Mystery titles by
GRETCHEN SPRAGUE

DEATH IN GOOD COMPANY
MAQUETTE FOR MURDER

MURDER IN A
HEAT WAVE

GRETCHEN
SPRAGUE

W❂RLDWIDE.

TORONTO • NEW YORK • LONDON
AMSTERDAM • PARIS • SYDNEY • HAMBURG
STOCKHOLM • ATHENS • TOKYO • MILAN
MADRID • WARSAW • BUDAPEST • AUCKLAND

To Elmer, Emily, and Tim

MURDER IN A HEAT WAVE

A Worldwide Mystery/April 2004

First published by St. Martin's Press.

ISBN 0-373-26489-9

Printed in U.S.A.

Acknowledgments

Thanks to Frank and Ursula Karelsen for information about and insights into high-rise co-op life and law in Manhattan, and to my agent, Maureen Moran, for more of the same and for other valuable advice and service.

ONE

Heat Wave

NEW YORK CITY IS apt to go to extremes, and on Wednesday, June 6, it was doing so again. At 10 p.m., when Martha Patterson joined the taxi line outside the United terminal at Kennedy, both the temperature and the humidity still hung in the middle eighties.

The taxi she drew was not air-conditioned.

Never mind; she was on the last leg of her daylong journey home, and her high-rise building, built in the 1950s to the dismay of Greenwich Villagers sensitive to architectural compatibility, had central air-conditioning. She cranked down the taxi window to let the exhaust fumes of the Belt Parkway fan her face, closed her eyes, and drifted back into the semi-doze that had relieved the tedium of the transcontinental flight. Grandchildren were all very well, and Martha was appropriately fond of hers, but when one has been free of child-rearing for upwards of two decades, prolonged exposure to the exuberance and self-involvement of the young can be exhausting. Martha had been visiting her son Robert and his family in California for ten days.

ONLY PARTIALLY ROUSED from her torpor by the cab's arrival at her destination, Martha almost failed to recognize the doorman who came out to the curb to help with her luggage. At this hour of the night, it should be Boris, but this man was not wearing his uniform jacket.

The blocky form and square face and the familiar, precisely enunciated "Good evening, Ms. Patterson," however, reassured her; this personage, however unjacketed, was indeed Boris. She had never particularly liked the man, whose difficult standards of decorum she had from time to time breached, but Boris's code of appropriate behavior had become a fixed point in her life, and his present departure from absolute sartorial correctness startled her.

"Good evening, Boris," she responded, and, as they mounted the shallow steps to the concrete plaza that fronted the building, took the liberty of adding, "Are you well?"

"I am, thank you. And you?"

"I'm well, thanks. Glad to be home."

"And we're very glad to have you home. But I'm sorry to say…" Boris was facing away from her and speaking quietly, so Martha lost the end of the sentence.

Its import, however, soon became clear. The entrance door was propped open, and when she passed through, she discovered that the lobby was as muggy as the street. What Boris had been sorry to say was, "The air conditioner is out of order."

WAITING FOR the elevator with her luggage at her feet, Martha found that jet lag was combining with the heat to elevate what had previously been moderate annoyance into something dangerously like curmudgeonly resentment. For years, a little grove of potted ficus trees had shielded the elevators and the mailboxes from the main body of the lobby. A recent redecoration, completed a few weeks before her trip, had removed the trees and substituted an openwork brass screen. Ficus, it seemed, had gone out of fashion. Martha had been missing the little trees ever since they had disappeared, but never more than tonight; living greenery would have blunted, however slightly, the edge of discomfort.

She was trying to adjust her attitude to something more appropriate to homecoming when she was joined in front of the elevator door by a slim blondish woman, a stocky red-haired man, and a leggy little girl asleep in the man's arms. Jeff and Vanessa Callaghan, and the child had a name like Tiffany—not actually Tiffany, but something out of the same box. Harmony? Not quite. Melody, that was it. They lived on the floor below hers, in the same wing of the building, and consequently used the same elevator.

All three were wearing shorts and T-shirts. Sweat soaked Jeff's underarms and beaded his flushed face. The little girl's fair hair clung to her scalp in damp curling tendrils. Vanessa looked relatively dry, but her mouth was petulant. Martha had concluded some time ago, however, that a pout was Vanessa Callaghan's normal expression and did not necessarily indicate her emotional state at any given time.

Martha said, "Good evening."

Vanessa said, "Hi," and pressed the up button, which Martha had already pressed. "Been away?"

"San Francisco."

"I'll bet you had decent weather there."

They had, in fact, had a good deal of fog. "It was pleasant," Martha said.

"And you come back to this." Jeff shifted the sleeping child's weight from one arm to the other. "I mean, do you believe this? Those turkeys assess us up the wazoo for that crap," the motion of his head took in the redecorated lobby on the other side of the screen, "and then they screw up our sale so we can't get out of here, and *now* they can't even maintain the plant."

They. The universal villain. But this, Martha knew, was a specific, identifiable *they.* The building was a co-op, and *they* were the seven members of the board of directors. "How long has the air conditioner been out of order?" she asked.

"Six days. Six...friggin'—"

"Jeff," said Vanessa.

"—days, and every damn one of them over ninety. Tell me about global warming. I mean, how many movies can you go to? That friggin' crew ought to be shot."

"Jeff, shush."

"She's asleep; she can't hear me."

"You don't know that."

"Listen, I mean it. If those turkeys can't maintain the plant, we ought to shoot the whole damn crew and get some new blood on the board."

"Jeff, stop it."

The child squirmed, made a small puppyish sound, and settled again.

Martha kept her voice soft. "Why not just elect a new board?"

"Been there. You know how it goes. Maybe ten people show up, and the old crew gets rubber-stamped by the proxies."

WELL, MARTHA CONCEDED, cranking open every window in her apartment, he had a point. Not, of course, about shooting the board, but certainly about the elections. Martha was one of the "maybe ten"—actually it was more like seventeen—who regularly attended the annual shareholders' meetings. They tended to be discontented shareholders, there to vote in person for opposing candidates. The other residents—those of them who troubled to vote at all—stayed away from the meetings and exercised their proxies in favor of "the old crew."

The open windows were not dispelling the heat. Martha owned two fans, but they were in her storage locker in the basement, and she was too tired to traipse down to fetch them. She undressed, stood for some time under a tepid shower, powdered herself lavishly, and made herself lie motionless on her bed.

A HUMIDITY-INDUCED headache woke her at 8 a.m., which would be five in the morning where she had come from. The temperature in the apartment had not dropped more than a couple of degrees, and no air moved through the open windows.

But she was home, and the day awaited her attention, so after aspirin, tea, and toast had somewhat restored her energy (she had prudently stored half a loaf in the freezer before leaving), she put on a sleeveless blouse, a mid-calf-length cotton skirt, and sandals, pocketed her keys, and set out to retrieve her fans. Fourteen years before, sometime around her sixtieth birthday, Martha had stopped exposing her legs to public view. They were still serviceable legs, barring a touch of arthritis in the knees, but what with spider veins, age spots, and a general inexplicable lumpiness, they no longer met American standards of comeliness. She had donated her shorts to the Salvation Army, and had then been surprised to find that loosely cut skirts, even long ones, were cooler than shorts, since they allowed air to circulate all the way up to the crotch.

The stairs and the service elevator, which provided access to the basement, were reached via a fire door at the far end of the corridor. Martha pushed through into the stairwell, summoned the service elevator, rode down, and pushed through another fire door into a concrete corridor. It was cooler down there, and a series of clattering bangs from the boiler room, which was located around a right-angle turn twenty or so feet farther along, raised the hope that repairs to the air conditioner were under way.

A different sort of rumbling told her that the laundry

room was in use. She glanced in when she reached the door and saw a woman in shorts and T-shirt sitting on a bench in the middle of the room. A clipboard was on her lap, a pencil was in her hand, and papers were stacked on the bench beside her. The woman looked up, and Martha recognized Ruth Kaplowitz, an upstairs neighbor.

"Oh, you're back," Ruth said. "Good, we need to talk."

Martha, who was seldom averse to talk, and particularly not with a neighbor as agreeable as Ruth Kaplowitz, ventured into the damp heat and sat down on the bench next to the pile of papers.

"This heat must be a shock," Ruth said. Perhaps it was inevitable that any conversation would begin with the heat.

"Rather," said Martha. "Boris seems to feel that he has failed in his duty."

"It isn't Boris who failed." Ruth stuck the pencil behind her ear. "I don't want to add to your jet lag, but I have a favor to ask."

Martha voiced a noncommittal *"Mm?"*

"It's about the board," said Ruth. "This air-conditioner failure has stirred up sentiment for a change, and a few of us are trying to put together a plan. We're having a little meeting tonight to see if we can organize a campaign. Can I interest you in joining us?"

An early bedtime would have interested Martha more, but organized action deserved to be encouraged. "Is it to be a nonviolent plan?" she asked.

Ruth smiled. "Have you been talking to Jeff Callaghan?"

"Within moments of my return. One does feel a certain sympathy, of course."

"Well, Jeff will be there. We're going to try to redirect some of that passion. I do hope you'll come. We could use your voice of reason."

Martha noted that her vanity was being stroked. She chose not to resist. "Yes," she said. "Yes, I'll come."

"Oh, good. Eight o'clock tonight, in our apartment."

TWO

Insurrection

RUTH HAD SAID, "A few of us." *Few,* Martha found, meant *eight.* Five women and three men, dressed for the tropics, were gathered around the Kaplowitzes' dining table, which was doing duty as a conference table. Their perspiring bodies contributed their own heat and humidity to the already oppressive atmosphere. The sun was going down, but the temperature wasn't; the air-conditioning still wasn't working; and the sluggish breeze that crept through the wide-open windows provided only intermittent relief. A couple of fans oscillating in the corners did what they could, which wasn't much.

Martha knew all the participants, at least by sight. She was best acquainted with the Kaplowitzes, a matched pair in their mid-forties with strong faces and curly dark hair, cropped short in Ruth's case, receding in Simeon's. Martha knew that they had two sons, the younger one now about eight years old, the older one just starting to cope with a cracking voice and a growth spurt; but the boys were in evidence only through the muffled beeps and rat-a-tats of an electronic game being played behind a closed door in the rear of the apartment. Martha suspected that this entertainment was allowed only in moderation, for the Kaplowitzes were overtly intellectual. Simeon was an associate professor of English literature at New York University. Ruth had held a similar position before they had adopted the older boy; now she worked at home as a freelance copy editor. When the younger boy had started school, she had also gone back to teaching, meeting a couple of evening classes at NYU's School of Continuing Education. The apartment walls were lined with bookshelves.

Martha knew the others less well. Jeff Callaghan was there, of course. The third man was a transplanted Englishman named Everett Upton, whom she knew because they had a friend in common. She invariably identified him in her thoughts as The Man with the Terrible Toupee. The hairpiece was patently false, of a uniform, youthful dark brown that emphasized by contrast the facial lines and furrows of late middle age. Martha knew vaguely that he was involved with the arts, not as a maker, but as a commentator, critic, reviewer—something along those lines. She had never understood how anyone with an eye for the aesthetic could present himself so unaesthetically. Everett had apologized for his wife's failure to attend: her health was precarious at the best of times, and the heat had laid her low. Wiping her damp forehead with a tissue, Martha thought that a reputation for vaguely defined ill health had its uses.

She had occasionally seen but had never met the

woman sitting next to her, who was now introduced as Karen Higgins. She had apparently come directly from an office, for she was dressed for summer success in a sleeveless, V-necked ecru dress that blended satisfactorily with her smooth café-au-lait complexion.

Filling out the roster were Bird Buckley, a tall woman with cropped hair and muscular arms and legs that were displayed to full advantage by shorts and tank top, and her roommate, Nadine Jones, a small, bulkily pregnant young woman in a pale-blue spaghetti-strapped tent, who if not pregnant would resemble a bird more closely than did her partner.

Half an hour into the meeting, Martha realized that unless someone took the lead in what the managing partner of her former law firm had termed "prioritizing the issues" eight people would have cooped themselves up in an un-air-conditioned apartment on a New York summer night for nothing more productive than listening to Jeff Callaghan's insistent and uninterruptible voice. Jeff had a pet peeve, and no one had been able to move him off it. By half past eight, it was only Martha's highly developed sense of civic responsibility that prevented her from fleeing to her own apartment and immersing herself in a tub of cool water.

Jeff's grievance could have been stated briefly. The Callaghans wanted to move. Selling their apartment in this building was, of course, a necessary prerequisite to purchasing something else to move into. After showing it for months, they had finally found someone willing to purchase their apartment at a figure close to their asking price, but just last Tuesday, the co-op board had refused to approve the prospective purchasers. Jeff blamed Arnold Stern, the president of the board, for orchestrating the refusal. Blamed him loudly and at length.

Ruth had suggested that Martha might help control Jeff. So far, however, neither Ruth nor Simeon had succeeded in providing her with an opportunity to help. They were sitting in what should be controlling positions at opposite ends of the table, but beyond uttering an occasional courteous and ineffective "Jeff…," neither of them was making any progress toward damming the flow.

"Help," Martha perceived, was to be translated as "Do it yourself."

So be it. Eventually Jeff had to draw a breath, and into that moment of quiet, Martha said, more loudly than she customarily spoke, "It can't be Arnold alone who disapproves. It takes a majority of the board to take action."

"Arnold," said Jeff, "always gets a majority."

"Then he must provide the board with plausible reasons."

"Huh?"

"What reason did the board give for disapproving your purchasers?"

"They *said* financial stability."

"Which is an appropriate ground for disapproving a purchaser."

"It's bullshit. They had mortgage approval."

Martha was well aware that it took more than mortgage approval to establish financial stability, but while she was trying to formulate a rebuttal that wouldn't be unduly provocative, Jeff barreled on. "Arnold just doesn't want a mixed-race couple with three tan kids right under him when he's trying to sell his place," he said, "but they couldn't say that."

"They almost did," said Karen Higgins. "'Financial stability' can be code for minority."

"But *you* live here," said Nadine.

Jeff said, "She doesn't live near Arnold."

With the floor now apparently open to discussion, Nadine persisted. "How do you know that's the reason? Did someone say something racial at the interview?"

"There wasn't any interview," said Jeff. "They turned them down on the paperwork."

"That doesn't make sense," said Nadine. "If there wasn't any interview, how would the board know what color they were?"

"Someone must have seen them when they were here viewing the apartment."

Martha's lawyer persona protested. "Must have" is not evidence. "Perhaps," she suggested, "the reason really was their financial situation."

"I told you, they had mortgage approval."

Once more Martha rejected the impulse to outline the elements of financial stability. Further wrangling would be profitless.

Karen Higgins, however, wasn't ready to let the subject drop. "Maybe something slipped out at the meeting," she said. "Have you looked at the minutes?"

"Yeah, right—"

"Jeff," said Simeon.

"—like they'd let anything like that get into the minutes."

Karen said, "But it wouldn't hurt to look."

"The sacred minutes? Just try—"

"But…"

Martha closed her eyes and summoned a vision of snowcapped mountains. Maybe she could convert these rancorous voices into the rush of a waterfall….

A sharp *crack* jerked her eyes open. The formidably muscular Bird Buckley had slapped her hand on the table. *"Jeff!"* she snapped. "Give it a *rest*. Nobody's going to vote out that board just because they disapproved your sale."

Martha had the illusion that Jeff's hair had turned redder. "Whadda you mean, *just?*" he snarled.

"Jeff," said Simeon.

Jeff ignored him. "Whadda you mean, *just* because? Arnold Stern is screwing up my life. The man's a friggin' tyrant." He glowered across the table at Karen. "A friggin' *racist* tyrant."

Martha looked at her watch. It was nearly nine o'clock. Her gaze crossed Simeon's. He raised his eyebrows, miming helplessness. Her options were clear: take control or go home.

But home, she decided, wasn't really an option. It was still too early to retreat.

She glared across the table at Jeff and, emulating to the best of her ability the most intimidating judge she had ever appeared before, said, "That is enough."

Jeff blinked.

"Hear, hear," said Everett Upton. They were the first words he had uttered since apologizing for his wife's absence.

"It is time to move on," said Martha.

"Right on," said Simeon, looking relieved.

Jeff opened his mouth. Martha stared at him. He closed his mouth, folded his arms, and transferred his gaze to the wall behind her head.

When she was reasonably certain that he was going to remain silent, she said, "I was given to understand that we've come here to discuss getting some new blood on the board."

"Hear, hear," said Everett again.

Jeff, not entirely silenced, muttered. "Shoot 'em all."

"Oh, just be quiet," said pregnant little Nadine Jones. "That isn't the kind of blood we're talking about."

"Only kind that would work."

"Man," said Karen Higgins, "you better watch your mouth. What if somebody goes and does it?"

"Buy him a drink."

"Yeah, right. And then the police come around, and people say, 'Hey, what about that Jeff fellow? Him with the red hair and the big mouth. He was talking about shooting those clowns. Go find out what he was doing on, you know, the night of.' Last I heard, Sing Sing wasn't air-conditioned."

"They'd give me a medal."

"In the city, maybe, everybody's living in co-ops

and hate their boards. So they say they can't get an unbiased jury, and they move your trial out where everybody lives in their own little house in their own little yard and nobody ever heard of co-op boards.''

"Ha ha, funny," said Bird. "Now can we get to the point? If we're going to get rid of the board, we have to vote them out. So who do we run, and how do we get out the vote?"

"Hear, hear," said Everett.

Simeon said, "The failure to maintain the air conditioner should get out the vote."

"And the redecoration of the lobby," said Ruth.

"I don't want to be a pest," said Karen Higgins, "but I don't know if the lobby would fly. Some people like it."

On topic at last.

Martha closed her eyes and assigned her ears the responsibility for paying attention. Like waves lapping at a beach, voices flowed in and ebbed back, leaving words settling like jetsam on packed wet sand. "Air conditioner," she heard, and "maintenance"—eventually "priorities."

Misplaced had just beached next to *priorities* when a telephone warbled behind a closed door. She identified the rustle of Ruth's getting to her feet and leaving the room.

Karen Higgins's voice registered loud and clear: "Misplaced priorities. I like it."

A generalized murmur bore the upward tone of agreement.

Martha opened her eyes and saw Simeon wink at her. He had noticed her brief quasi-nap.

Then Ruth appeared in the archway to the back hall. "Mr. Upton," she said, "there's a Peter Sanders on the phone for you."

"Oh, dear," said Everett. He got to his feet and went out, and Ruth sat down.

Simeon said, "I think we have a platform. Misplaced priorities."

"Sounds good," said Ruth.

"Next subject," said Simeon. "Who's going to stand on this platform?"

"Great question," said Bird Buckley. "Where do we find seven victims?"

"Only three," Simeon said. He rustled through some papers in front of him. "The terms are staggered. George Wilkins, Helen Taubensee, and Philip Schwartz are up for reelection this year.

"Hold on!" Jeff came abruptly out of his slump. "Are you saying—?"

But just then Everett Upton reappeared, and the group's attention abandoned Jeff.

"Frightfully sorry," Everett said, "but I must leave. Please carry on."

"Bad news?" asked Ruth.

"Not good. My friend Irene Xendopoulis is having a medical crisis. Do carry on."

CARRYING ON, of course, was precisely what Jeff had in mind. "Are you telling us we can't get rid of Arnold?" he demanded.

"Not this year," said Simeon.

"What the hell are we doing here if we can't get rid of Arnold?"

"Don't raise your voice." Ruth nodded toward the floor, reminding them all that Arnold Stern's apartment was directly below the Kaplowitzes'. (It was also, although the fact was irrelevant to present circumstances, directly above the Callaghans' and next door to Martha's. Arnold was, so to speak, the ham in a sandwich of discontent, and Martha, perhaps, was a side order of slaw.)

"Yolanda Young, too," said Nadine Jones.

"Is she any more important than the others?" Ruth asked as she sat down.

"You don't know?" said Nadine.

"Enlighten me."

"She's the one who pushed through the lobby renovation."

"How do you know that?"

"She's an interior designer. It stands to reason."

"But she didn't have the lobby contract, did she? I should think that would be a conflict of interest."

"No, but I'll bet she got a kickback."

Martha's lawyer persona stirred again. "Unless you have evidence," she said, "I'd be careful about accusing someone of criminal activity."

Nadine blinked. "I'm not accusing," she said. "I'm just...you know..."

"*Do* you have any evidence?" asked Simeon.

"Just, you know, she was pushing it every time she opened her mouth. But that isn't really my point. My point is, with Arnold running the board, it just seems to work out that whatever Yolanda wants, Yolanda gets, so she'd be a good person to get rid of, too.''

''Do they have a thing going?'' Jeff was interested once more.

''She didn't say that,'' said Bird.

''Well, what the hell was she saying?''

''Just listen, would you?'' said Nadine. ''What I'm saying is, the woman wants bad things and Arnold gets them for her.''

''Give me a f'r instance.''

Nadine said, ''Number one, *as* I said, *if* you'd listen, she wanted the lobby done and the board did the lobby. Number two, she didn't like the way we wanted to divide up our space to make a nursery for the baby, and the board turned down our renovation. *After* they approved that woman's alterations....''

''What woman?''

''That Irene whosis, down on the second floor. The one our Brit friend just left to take care of. I don't know why she called him and not Arnold. She and Arnold are like *this*.'' Nadine held up crossed fingers.

''Yolanda whatsis and Irene whosis, both?'' Jeff said. ''Arnold must be a busy man.''

''Not the same thing. Irene's about seventy....'' Nadine looked at Martha. ''I didn't mean that the way it sounded. I mean it's just, they're friends. Real good friends. So when this good friend of Arnold's wanted to tear up a bunch of walls so she could use a wheelchair, they approved it, and then, when *Yolanda* didn't like our plan for a nursery, Arnold took against it....''

"Hold it!" said Karen Higgins. "We're staying out of private stuff, okay?"

"I'm just making the point. Whatever Yolanda wants, Yolanda gets, and one of the things she wants is to mess up our lives."

"A lot of assumptions there," said Simeon. "What if Arnold approved of the lobby work and disapproved of your renovation plans on his own, independently of Yolanda Young?"

"Dream on," said Nadine. "She's just determined to mess up our lives, and I wish we could get her off the board."

"She might be easier to beat than Arnold," said Karen. "He has that, you know, that aura. Like he knows what he's doing."

"So what?" Jeff was rapidly sinking back into his sulk. "We can't get rid of either one of them."

"Well, we won't get rid of anyone if we give up before we start," said Karen. "When's the election?"

"The week after Labor Day," said Simeon.

"That should give us time to organize. So who's going to run? How about you, Bird? Nadine? One of you get on the board and build your nursery."

Conflict of interest, muttered Martha's lawyer persona.

But Bird said, "We're going to be busy with the baby. How about you?"

"Well, I would, but I'm really busy at work," said Karen, "and anyway, I don't know that a woman of color would be the best person to start with. I'll sure help."

An old bedtime story called "The Little Red Hen" began playing itself in Martha's head. When Robert was four years old, he had insisted on having it read to him, night after night, for months.

"Who will plant the corn?" asked the little red hen. "Not I," said the dog. "Not I," said the cat....

"Jeff?" said Karen.

Good heavens, she must be joking.

"My plate's full," Jeff said.

"Not I," said the rooster. Good.

"Anyway, I get mad too easy," Jeff added, displaying a level of self-knowledge that surprised Martha. "I'd probably end up shooting the whole crew."

"Jeff," said Karen, "do you actually have a gun to go with that mouth of yours?"

"With a kid in the house? No way."

"Too bad," said Simeon. "Arnold does."

Martha's eyes, which had closed again, jerked open. "He does?" she said. "I didn't know that."

"He showed it to me," said Simeon. "Now if Jeff just had one, they could shoot it out at the OK Corral and you could all go home."

"Simeon," said Ruth. "Unfunny."

"You're right," Simeon said. "I'm sorry."

"Right here in the building," said Nadine. "That is scary."

"And you live ten floors down," said Simeon. "How do you think I feel, my family up here on top of the thing? He suggested that I get one."

"You didn't!" said Nadine.

"Of course not."

"I think we should make it a campaign issue," Nadine said. "Prohibit guns in the building."

"And as soon as we raise the issue, the NRA'll fund their campaign," said Simeon.

"And speaking of campaigns," said Ruth.

A sudden silence fell. People shifted in their chairs.

"It's a big commitment, I know," said Ruth.

"Three," said Bird.

More silence.

"Actually," Simeon said, "one new board member could make a difference, if it's a strong character."

Martha glanced across the corner of the table. Simeon was looking at her. "If you're volunteering," she said, "I'd support that." She doubted that he was volunteering.

He wasn't. "I appreciate the compliment," he said, "but I think somebody who works at home would be more in touch with the voters."

"Ruth," she said. Very likely he didn't mean Ruth, either.

"I'd do it in a minute," Ruth said, "but the board meetings are in the evening, and that's when I meet classes."

Not I, said the horse, not I, said the cow. Not that Ruth Kaplowitz was in any way bovine. Martha said, "It's evening now, and you're here."

"I'm not teaching summer school, but I'll be back in harness in September."

Simeon was still looking at Martha. "You'd be ideal, you know."

She had suspected it was coming.

While she was preparing a protest, Karen Higgins said, "Sounds good to me."

"Ideal," echoed Ruth. "You were living here when the building went co-op, so you know the ins and outs, and I've never heard of anybody putting anything over on you."

Nadine and Bird made assenting noises. Even Jeff, his arms still folded, nodded.

So Martha had been cast as the little red hen. And yes, at some level of awareness, she had seen it coming. It had not only been coming; it had been set up. The dog and the cat and the rooster and the horse and the cow having declined, Martha was supposed to say, *Then I will.*

"I don't believe...," she began, but the telephone rang once more, and Ruth got up and disappeared into the back hall, and Martha's demurral was lost.

Jeff had stopped sulking. "You'll be reasonable about buyers, right?"

"We'll resubmit our renovation plan," said Nadine, stroking her belly. "And let's really think about banning guns."

Simeon leaned toward Martha and muttered sotto voce, "And you can repeal the dog rule."

"The what?"

"Could we be happy without a private grievance? Don't worry about it."

Ruth reappeared. "For you," she said to Martha. "Everett Upton."

THREE

Emergency

EVERETT SOUNDED both rattled and apologetic, but decidedly more rattled than apologetic. He was frightfully sorry to be troubling her.

Only too glad for a break from conspiracy, Martha said, "Not at all. You're not troubling me at all. What's wrong?"

"It's Irene. She's having rather a bad asthma attack, and her inhaler isn't doing the job. She's using her oxygen, but even so, she can scarcely breathe. We've sent for an ambulance."

Irene was Irene Xendopoulis, a retired archaeologist who was plagued with a complex of pulmonary and neurological ailments that required the occasional use of an oxygen tank and would eventually confine her to a wheelchair. While not quite a friend of Martha's, she was at least a very friendly acquaintance, good for amusingly acerbic conversation during chance meetings in the laundry room.

"How can I help?" Martha asked.

"If you wouldn't mind—she needs help dressing. She's refusing to go out in her nightgown, and she won't permit Peter or me to help her dress. I should have thought a dressing gown would be perfectly adequate, but—well—you know how she can be.''

Yes, Martha knew how Irene could be: independent to the point of stubbornness. She lived alone in a one-bedroom apartment down on the second floor. A visiting nurse attended her twice a week. Irene deplored her need for even that degree of assistance.

Everett said, "I thought…if you wouldn't mind terribly…''

Martha didn't mind terribly. She didn't mind at all. She had no trouble understanding the residual vanity, however misguided, that made an elderly woman reluctant to display her body to male view. "I'll be right down,'' she said.

THE SLUGGISH air currents that had crept through the Kaplowitzes' eighteenth-floor windows failed altogether down here on the second floor. The apartment was stifling. Martha herself, blessed with healthy lungs, felt half-smothered as soon as she stepped through the door.

A dark-haired young man was pacing the living-room floor. Everett hastily introduced him as Irene's nephew, Peter Sanders, and then directed Martha to the bedroom where Irene, dressed only in a sweat-soaked nightgown, was sitting on the edge of the bed. Tubes taped to her nostrils ran to a green oxygen tank beside the bed. Even with that help, each breath was an audible struggle.

"Aah," she sighed past the obstructions. "You came."

"Of course."

"Like a good…neighbor…" Even breathless, Irene managed to whisper the first couple of bars of the State Farm Insurance commercial.

"Maybe," Martha suggested, too tense for amusement, "you should save your strength for this project."

Irene nodded. The movement dislodged one of the breathing tubes. She pressed the tape back into place and whispered, "To work."

And work it was. Irene was by no means a sylph, and she needed support just to raise her hips far enough to remove the nightgown and drag on underpants and after them a skirt. Martha shrugged an incipient cramp from her shoulders before proceeding to bra and blouse, which, requiring no lifting, were easier. Irene chose not to wear stockings, for which Martha was grateful, but she declined to go barefoot. Buckling her sandals entailed kneeling. Martha's knees complained, but that was nothing new, and when at last Irene deemed herself sufficiently decent to venture into public view, the stress on Martha's aging joints ended. She retrieved Irene's handbag from the clutter on top of the bureau, pulled a tissue from a box on the nightstand, wiped her face, and summoned the men.

Peter, the nephew, removed a folding wheelchair from the closet, opened it, and hoisted Irene into it. Everett pushed her out of the bedroom while Peter steered the oxygen tank behind them on its wheeled rack.

In the corridor, Irene fished a ring of keys from her handbag. Martha locked the apartment and gave the keys back to Irene. She meant to see the little procession into the elevator and then wait for its return to carry her up to her sanctuary on the seventeenth floor.

But Irene disoriented her by closing a hand over her wrist and wheezing, ''What's…happening?''

''Happening?'' Martha stalled. Surely the men had informed Irene that they were taking her to the hospital.

Irene tilted her head upward. ''Meeting.''

Oh. The gathering in the Kaplowitzes' apartment.

This interest in something besides her struggling lungs was surely to be encouraged. Martha said, ''A congress of conspirators.''

A frown puckered Irene's forehead. ''Kick out… board?''

The frown reminded Martha that the insurrection might not be the best possible topic of conversation; the board had recently done what Irene wanted.

''It's being discussed,'' she hedged.

Irene was not easily put off. ''Arnold?'' she demanded.

Arnold. Irene's friend. Close as crossed fingers. Again Martha equivocated. ''He isn't up for reelection this year.''

''Next…year?''

Avoidance simply wasn't working. ''His term expires next year,'' Martha said. ''It's not clear if anyone will run against him then.''

''Someone should do,'' said Everett, ''or our impetuous young colleague may carry out his threat.''

''Threat?'' Irene twisted to look at him and dislodged a breathing tube. She thrust it back into place. ''Threat?''

''A redheaded young chap named Jeffrey Callaghan,'' said Everett. ''He recommends shooting as a remedy for grievances.''

''Shooting…Arnold?''

''The whole crew, actually.'' Everett was obviously enjoying himself.

Annoyed, Martha said, ''He's just blowing off steam,'' and then the elevator arrived.

She planted her foot in the track to hold the door open while Everett and Peter coordinated their maneuvers. When they were safely inside, she removed her foot and the door began to slide shut in front of her.

But Irene said, ''No, come along,'' and Peter whacked the edge of the door with the flat of his hand to reverse its direction.

Obediently, Martha edged in. Peter took his hand away, and the door closed behind her. As they started down, Everett said, ''One doesn't like to be alarmist, but I do wonder about that blowing-off-steam theory. One thinks of those frightful school massacres. Their threats were ignored, and one sees what happened.''

''Jeff Callaghan isn't a disturbed schoolboy,'' said Martha.

"All the same, I rather think Arnold should be warned."

"Jeff doesn't have a gun."

"Can one be certain?"

Once more annoyed, and annoyed all the more for knowing that annoyance was unreasonable, Martha said, "Yolanda Young is also being accused of messing up people's lives. Perhaps she should be warned, as well."

"Oh, indeed? Whose life is she, aah, 'messing up'?" Everett's voice inserted quotation marks around the phrase.

"It must have come up after you left," Martha said. "Those two young women want to remodel their apartment to make a nursery. The board disapproved their plan, and they claim it was Yolanda Young who engineered the opposition."

The elevator stopped. With no further comment from Everett, they emerged into the lobby.

Boris was once more in shirtsleeves. "Your ambulance hasn't arrived," he said.

Everett gave vent to an irritated *"Tchk,"* and bent over the wheelchair. "I'm going to get my car," he said. "If the ambulance comes first, just go on."

THEY WAITED INSIDE the entrance door. It was on the side of the building and opened on a plaza, a landscaped open space between this building and the next. Its position allowed someone inside the glass doors to see about half a block up the street. Martha found herself craning her neck in a futile effort to see farther.

An arm's length away from her, Peter was holding his own vigil.

Irene wheezed some words that Martha didn't quite catch. She dragged her attention back from the street and said, "I'm sorry?"

"Are you running...for...board?"

What could have given Irene the idea? Had the conspirators been polling the building before the meeting? "I don't know," she said. "I've been asked, but I'm not enchanted with the idea."

"Do it."

"What's your agenda?"

"Agenda?"

"Everyone has a private agenda. They were ostensibly concerned about building-wide issues like the air-conditioning and the lobby, but most of them were primarily concerned with private grievances."

"Such as?"

"Oh, approve our buyers, approve our renovation, repeal the dog rule. That kind of thing."

"Whose buyer?"

"The Callaghans'. Their latest one was turned down. I'm to approve the next one, if any. And the two women are having a baby—I told you this already."

"Nursery."

"Just so. They claim the board is messing up their lives. Actually, they developed another item during the meeting. They propose amending the bylaws to ban guns."

"Guns?"

"I'd be inclined to support that one. It seems my next-door neighbor has one."

"Arnold."

"You know about it?"

"Showed me. They want…ban?"

"Ban guns, remove ban on dogs."

"Dogs? Oh!" Irene strained forward. "Peter?"

He turned away from the door. "Here," he said.

Irene rummaged in her handbag. "Forgot…allergy…" She pulled out the keys, closed her eyes, and strained to draw a breath. "Medi—"

"You want me to get your allergy medicine?"

Irene shook her head impatiently. "List."

Peter frowned.

Martha ventured a guess: "The list of medications you're allergic to?"

Irene nodded carefully and jingled the keys. "Desk. Middle…right."

"It's in the middle right-hand drawer of your desk?"

Another nod.

Peter's face cleared. "Got it." He took the keys and sprinted for the elevator.

"Oh." Her neck corded with tension, Irene gasped, "Pe—ter."

Nearly to the elevators, he turned.

"It's…all right," wheezed Irene.

Peter hesitated for a moment; then he said, "Good," and disappeared around the screen.

What, Martha wondered, was that cryptic exchange about? Did Peter himself know what was "all right"?

She rather doubted that he did; his good had sounded more like a concession to a sick old aunt than an indication of comprehension.

But Irene seemed content.

AND STILL they waited.

And at last Martha heard the warbling howl they'd been waiting for, faint but growing above the constant white noise of the city; and after a moment the ambulance appeared, shouldering its way along the street, lights flashing, siren blaring, its white bulk edging past cars that should have moved aside but couldn't, for where on the streets of New York City is there room to move aside?

It pulled up next to a fire hydrant, and as the siren moaned down to silence, two white-uniformed men and a white-uniformed woman jumped out and began unloading equipment. They were wheeling a gurney through the door when Peter Sanders, pale and agitated, came sprinting across the lobby with a sheet of paper in his hand.

FOUR

Decision

WHEN SHE WOKE UP up the next morning, Martha found that much of her jet lag had dissipated. With Irene delivered into the hands of professionals and with none of the insurgents demanding that she decide forthwith about running for the co-op board, she turned on her computer and resumed her normal work schedule. She had undertaken her freelance retirement job, legal research and writing for small law firms whose caseloads exceeded their research capabilities, more to keep her brain from turning to Jell-O after retirement than for the income, so before the California trip, she had accepted only assignments with deadlines well in the future. Those deadlines were now approaching. On the whole, she was grateful; the obligation to work overrode the obligation to decide about running for the board.

She stuck to her workstation—the humidity stayed up, making *stuck* no mere figure of speech—for the rest of Friday and most of Saturday. Each day, when she broke for lunch, she called Patient Information. On both occasions, Patient Information asked her to spell

Xendopoulis, and then informed her that Patient Irene
Xendopoulis's condition was stable. On neither occasion did Patient Information inform her of the level of
health or debility at which Patient Xendopoulis's condition had stabilized.

On Sunday morning, she woke to a breeze through
her wide-open windows. A Canadian front had moved
in, temporarily removing the urgency from the air-
conditioning issue. She tried Patient Information once
more, with no better result than before, and at ten-
thirty she dialed Everett Upton's number. It was only
after his machine answered that she remembered that
the Uptons were churchgoers. She tabled her concern
about Irene and set about living her life, which on that
particular Sunday afternoon included lunch and a
chamber music concert with a friend.

When she returned late in the afternoon, the temperature was temperate and the humidity was unde-
tectable. She had just come up the shallow steps to the
plaza beside her building when two children shoved
out through the door and scampered to the far side of
the plaza. Ruth Kaplowitz followed them out. Thus
cued, Martha identified the boy, who was wearing
jeans and a T-shirt imprinted with the name and por-
trait of Derek Jeter, as Tyler, the younger of the Kaplowitzes' two sons. The other youngster was a blond
little girl in hot pink shorts and a matching T-shirt:
the Callaghans' daughter, Melody. That the children
were friends was made immediately evident by Tyler's
aiming a poke at Melody's ribs and shouting, "You're
bad!"

Melody shouted, "I'm *good!*" and jumped onto the concrete edging of one of the planters that bordered the plaza.

"Martha, hello," said Ruth. "Isn't this weather a relief?"

Tyler jumped onto the planter rim beside Melody. "You're *bad!*"

"Delightful," agreed Martha.

"I'm *good!*" Melody jumped down and ran back across the plaza, just managing to dodge a young man who was pushing out the door from the lobby. She jumped onto a planter beside the steps to the sidewalk and shouted, "I'm *good,* I'm *good,* I'm *good!*"

The young man, Martha realized after a moment, was Irene's nephew, Peter Sanders. Good. Here was a surer source of patient information than Patient Information.

"Good afternoon, Peter," she said.

He stopped as if jolted. His eyes focused. "Oh," he said. "Oh, Ms.…Ms. Patterson. Sorry, I…" He gestured distractedly with a zippered bag he was carrying.

His discomposure was ominous. With some trepidation, Martha asked, "How is your aunt?"

"Uh…" He glanced toward the street, then dragged his attention back. "Not good. She had a heart attack in the ambulance, and she's in intensive care."

"Oh, dear. Have they given you a prognosis?"

"Not really. They're being—you know—vague." He lifted the bag again. "I was just getting her some things."

Martha had experienced that physicianly vagueness during Edwin's final illness. It had driven her frantic.

Peter glanced once more toward the street. It would be a kindness to release him.

"I don't want to keep you," Martha said. "Please give her my best wishes."

"Yes," he said, "yes, thanks." He turned, bounded down the steps, and dashed away up the street, dodging through pedestrian traffic.

Melody jumped off the planter beside the steps and ducked behind Ruth.

Ruth said, "A relative of that friend of Everett's? Irene?"

"Her nephew," said Martha. "I'm sorry, I should have introduced you."

"Intensive care," said Ruth. "That's worrisome. Was it the heat, do you think?"

"I wouldn't be surprised. Her apartment was stifling. I suppose it's encouraging that she needs some things from home."

"I wonder if she'll sue. But I shouldn't bring that up. It'd be another headache for the board, and I don't want to discourage you. Have you had a chance to think about it?"

"I've dithered."

"I understand. It's a big commitment. But we need a lawyer on the board."

"They have their own lawyer."

"For all the good that does. They barge ahead without listening to him. You'd make them listen."

While Martha was searching for a response to that

naive expression of faith, Tyler wandered over from the far side of the plaza.

"Miz Patterson?" he murmured. His face was as earnest and guileless as a Norman Rockwell illustration.

"Yes?" Martha said.

As she spoke, someone else—a generic New York businesswoman in her mid-forties, carefully made up and seriously hair-styled—came out of the building and turned toward the street. Martha recognized her without actually knowing her. She had seen her most often at the front of the room at annual board meetings: Yolanda Young, the interior designer who had offended Bird and Nadine.

Tyler ignored her. "If you get on the board," he said to Martha, "would you please let us have a dog again?"

Yolanda Young glanced back over her shoulder. She had been only a few steps away; she could not have failed to overhear.

Not that it mattered. If Martha decided to run, everyone in the building would know.

But Tyler was waiting. If she got on the board, would she get the dog rule repealed?

More to the point, *could* she get the dog rule repealed? "*If* is a big word," she said.

Children hate *if*s; nevertheless, Tyler nodded. A patient child, thought Martha. "And it takes more than one person to change the rules," she added.

Tyler's patience was not infinite. "But...," he said.

"Tyler," said Ruth.

"No, it's all right," Martha said. "A constituent is entitled to ask. Tyler, I'll make you a promise. *If* I run, and *if* I get elected, I promise that I'll do all I can to change the dog rule."

Her first campaign promise. Teetering between amusement and dismay, she noted how politically she had burdened it with conditions.

But Tyler was a well-brought-up child, and it took only the slightest nudge on Ruth's part to produce a thank-you. Then Ruth took the children away, and Martha entered her building.

Having exchanged a few inconsequential phrases with the weekend doorman, who had been hired only recently and was manning the podium this afternoon for the first time without his supervisor at his elbow, she proceeded back past the bronze screen to the elevator and up to her apartment, and went straight back to her study and took down the dictionary from its shelf beside her desk.

She had called Tyler a constituent. But could someone who was not a candidate have constituents? If constituents belonged only to a candidate, an inaccurate choice of words might accidentally have committed her to running.

No, she had not misspoken: one meaning of *constituent* was "a resident of a constituency" and one meaning of *constituency* was "the residents of an electoral district." This building, ruled as it was by an elected board of directors, could reasonably be called an electoral district, and Tyler Kaplowitz was a resident of this building. He was, therefore, a constituent, whether or not she was a candidate.

Idiotically relieved, she replacéd the dictionary on the shelf. As she was doing so, she heard a thump on the wall behind her desk. It was the wall that her apartment shared with Arnold Stern's. Before she had left for California, Arnold had told her he planned to be away for this weekend. He must have returned.

The thump was too muffled to count as a disturbance, but she found herself resenting it anyway. It was a reminder of Arnold Stern's existence, and she didn't want to think about Arnold Stern. By avoiding controversial topics, Martha, and Edwin before his death, had coexisted amicably with the Sterns for fifteen years. Running for a seat on the board would threaten that equilibrium. Although she would not be running directly against Arnold, she would inevitably be taking issue with some actions he had initiated, supported, or at least failed to oppose. And just now, Arnold had plenty to try his patience; a few weeks ago, his wife had moved out. Martha had no idea how he would react to a political challenge on top of this personal difficulty.

Martha was no stranger to hostility; one does not spend five decades in the practice of law without antagonizing people. But ticking off one's next-door neighbor was not to be lightly undertaken; many and irksome were the varieties of harassment available to occupants of abutting apartments. What if, she thought with determined frivolity, he came after her with that gun she was supposed to ban?

Oh, enough of this. She scanned the Jane Austen collection on her bookshelf. *Emma,* that was the ticket. Her last rereading had been at least five years ago. *Emma,* and in due time, a grilled cheese sandwich, and a sliced tomato sprinkled with salt and pepper.

HER PHONE RANG while she was cleaning up after her little meal. A bit of jet lag having returned, she considered letting the machine take the call, but then, as usual, took it herself.

A generic New York businesswoman's voice said, "Yes, Ms. Patterson. Yolanda Young here."

Now what? "Yes, Ms. Young?" seemed a sufficiently noncommittal response.

"I hear you may be running for a seat on the board, and I thought maybe we could talk about it a little. A friendly talk, I hope. How about coming down for a cup of coffee?"

That hadn't taken long. "Now?" Martha asked.

"Yes, if you're free."

There seemed no reason to refuse, so Martha admitted that she was free. Perhaps, if the opportunity arose, she might campaign for a return of the ficus trees.

YOLANDA YOUNG'S apartment, as one might expect of an interior designer's personal space, was designed to a fare-ye-well. Draperies, carpet, and paint looked fresh and unlived-in. The living room was furnished in café-au-lait leather and the dining alcove in Scandinavian teak; the kitchen ran to quarry tile floor, polished granite countertops, and a hissing espresso machine.

Martha surrendered to the leather, accepted cappuccino, and agreed that they were to be "Yolanda" and "Martha." Yolanda settled at one end of a love seat and said that she would welcome someone of Martha's competence on the board.

Doubting that this assertion accurately represented inner conviction, Martha said, "Thank you."

"I suppose," Yolanda said, "your campaign will be making a big issue of the air conditioner."

"I suppose it would come up."

"People always blame the board for everything that goes wrong. The fact is, the breakdown wasn't our fault. We're planning to sue the maintenance company."

Revealing that plan was a tactical misstep. Martha had long deplored the board's predilection for engaging in unnecessary litigation: lawsuits, even when successful, were expensive, and in the end it was the shareholders who paid the legal bills.

She said, "Mm."

Yolanda seemed—or pretended—not to notice her skepticism. She said, "It's unfortunate that the outage lasted so long. When people are uncomfortable, they don't think clearly. Really unfortunate."

Unfortunate for them, thought Martha. *Fortunate for us.*

And then, as if she had spoken those words aloud, she heard what she had just thought: *Them. Us.*

Good heavens, she must have decided.

Contemplating the sneaky ways of the unconscious, she failed even to say "Mm."

It was the telephone that broke the little silence. It stood behind a narrow panel of bronze filigree on a serving bar that divided the kitchen from the living room, so after Yolanda said, "Excuse me," and carried her cappuccino glass to the bar and set it down and reached around the filigree screen to pick up the handset, Martha couldn't help hearing her end of the exchange. Not that there was much to hear: just "Hello," and "Yes, this is Ms. Young. Who's calling, please?" Then a silence; then Yolanda slammed down the handset. Then she picked it up again and punched in numbers. After another short silence, she said, "Arnold, call me," and replaced the handset.

"What is it?" asked Martha.

"It was some guy...." Yolanda's voice was wobbly and her face was chalky beneath the blusher. She came back and dropped heavily on the love seat. "Some guy... Oh, my God. I've just had a death threat."

For a moment, the words were nothing but meaningless noise. Real life didn't contain death threats. "What did he say?" Martha asked.

"He said, 'Stop messing up people's lives or you're going to die.'" Yolanda stared at her. "My God," she said, "what kind of people are you running with?"

"Excuse me?"

"Messing up people's lives. That's the way your crowd talks."

My crowd?

Us.

"It was a man?" Martha asked.

"What?"

"You said 'some guy.' It was a man making the call?"

Yolanda started to speak; then she hesitated, and her face went remote. After a moment she said, "I don't know."

"But you thought it was a man."

"I thought it was, but he didn't…he didn't sound… natural."

Remembered voices tumbled over each other in Martha's mind: *Shoot the whole crew. She's just determined to mess up our lives. Whatever Yolanda wants, Yolanda gets.*

"Could it have been someone trying to disguise his voice?" she asked. "Or hers?" she added.

"A woman? I don't know. Maybe."

Maybe implied *maybe not;* so maybe a man, after all.

Whatever Yolanda wants, Yolanda gets.

Arnold's wife had just left him.

"Do you want to notify the police?" Martha asked.

Yolanda got up from the love seat, paced restlessly to the serving bar, came back, sat down. "I don't see the point," she said at last. "What can I tell them? Someone I don't know said I should stop doing something I don't know I'm doing or I'm going to die, he didn't say how? She, whoever. What could the police do, tell me to get Caller ID? I'll do that without them telling me."

MARTHA LEFT without lobbying for the ficus. She hadn't forgotten; she had just decided, upon noticing that the little bronze screen that hid the telephone was filigreed in the same pattern as the big bronze screen that hid the elevators, that Yolanda Young had probably been the one responsible for getting rid of the trees.

FIVE

Twice

US, THOUGHT MARTHA as she rode the elevator back to the seventeenth floor.

What kind of people are you running with?
Stop messing up people's lives or you'll die.
Shoot the whole crew.

SHE OPENED *Emma* and stretched out on the chaise. Presently she realized that although her eyes were moving across the words, her mind wasn't absorbing their meaning.

Messing up our lives.

Bird Buckley and Nadine Jones had used those words.

What kind of people am I running with?

The answer wasn't hard. She was running with frustrated people. And elections had been invented to give frustrated people a nonviolent outlet for their frustration.

She slipped a bookmark between the pages of her book, looked up the Kaplowitzes' number, and punched it in.

Simeon answered.

Martha said, "Am I speaking to the chairman of the draft board?"

"We don't draft," he said without missing a beat. "We accept volunteers."

"You coerce volunteers."

"'Moral suasion' is the preferred term."

"No doubt. Simeon, I'm not sure I believe I'm doing this, but if you can get a campaign committee together, I'll run."

Simeon was silent for a moment.

Martha said, "Unless someone else has stepped forward."

"Oh, no. No, not at all. I was just suppressing a whoop of delight. The campaign committee shall be got together in a matter of hours. Well, days." Another pause. "I'm sure you know I'm glad. I hope you are."

"I hope so, too."

"Do I dare to ask what made up your mind?"

"Tyler's dog," she said.

SHE SLEPT WELL and in the morning settled into a concentrated spell of work that lasted all day. A little before five, the telephone interrupted the flow. She let the machine answer. "This is Rashida Grant at Lowell and Merling," said a woman's voice. "I'm trying—"

Lowell and Merling was the management firm that served Martha's building; Rashida Grant was one of those indispensable employees, less than an agent, far more than a secretary, without whom businesses would cease to function. Martha picked up.

"Hello, Ms. Grant," she said. "This is the real Martha Patterson."

"Oh, good. I hope you can help me. I'm trying to get hold of Arnold Stern, and nobody seems to know where he is. His school says he had an all-day meeting at the Board of Ed., the Board of Ed. says the meeting was over at three-thirty, the school says he didn't come back there, and his machine's picking up at home. Your name is on his emergency list, so now I'm bothering you."

Martha had nearly forgotten. Years ago, when Arnold and Lila Stern had moved into the apartment next door, they had designated the Pattersons as people to be notified in case of emergency. No emergency had ever before called for their notification.

"I know he was away for the weekend," she said. "I think he came home yesterday, but I haven't seen him. Would you like me to go and ring his doorbell?"

"Oh, that'd be great. Would you mind?"

"Not at all. It's just next door. Hold on; I'll try."

She put the phone on hold, went out and up the corridor to Arnold's door, pushed the doorbell button, waited, pushed again, waited again, pushed again. Nobody answered.

She went back to her phone and released HOLD. "He doesn't seem to be at home."

"Oh, shoot." A sigh gusted over the line. "He has some papers our lawyer needs. I'm going to have to go in his place to look for them, and I can't do it alone. Will you be there for the next hour or so?''

"Don't you have keys?"

"The keys aren't the problem. It's just, this isn't an entry for repair, so Mr. Palladino says I have to have somebody with me."

Did a lawyer's need for some undefined papers constitute an emergency? The lawyer would think so. "What kind of papers?" Martha asked.

"The maintenance contract for the air conditioner. The lawyer has a meeting with the air-conditioner people first thing tomorrow morning, and both copies are gone, ours and the lawyer's both. Mr. Stern was in here Friday, looking at it with the lawyer, and now we can't find it. He left in sort of a hurry, and Mr. Palladino thinks he probably bundled it in with his by mistake."

"Surely the air-conditioner people have a copy."

"The lawyer needs his own."

Yes, of course; it would be marked up with talking points. Martha said, "I shouldn't think it's likely to be in Mr. Stern's apartment. If he took it by accident, it would probably still be in his briefcase, and I should think he'd have his briefcase with him."

"That's what I think, but Mr. Palladino said to go look in his apartment."

Martha had no wish to enter Arnold Stern's apartment uninvited—or invited, for that matter. But her name was, after all, on his emergency-notification list, a circumstance that must provide some sort of right of entry, and in any case, her value system prohibited giving subordinate employees a hard time.

"All right," she said, "come on over. I'll enter his apartment with you so that if necessary, I can testify that you didn't abscond with any valuables. Is that what you need?"

"Yes, it is. Thank you. Thank you very much."

RASHIDA GRANT HAD a substantial build, an air of competence, and a ring of keys. Martha waited while she pushed Arnold's doorbell.

Nobody answered.

Rashida banged on the door with sturdy knuckles. No response.

Rashida looked at Martha. Martha nodded. Rashida said, "Okay, here goes nothin'."

The door had three locks: a Yale, a Medeco, and a police lock. The Yale and the Medeco yielded readily, but the police lock gave her a bit of trouble. When it finally gave way, she said, "Uh-oh. I don't think it was locked. I think the first time I turned the key, I was lockin' it. I hope that doesn't mean he's in here." She turned the knob. "In here with somebody'd be worse. I don't really want to be doing this." She pushed the door wide open and called, "Hel-looo!"

Nobody answered.

"OH, *NO!*" exclaimed Hannah Gold. Sixty miles of telephone connection failed to mute her distressed incredulity. "No, Martha, you didn't. You dreamed it."

"Hannah, don't do that," Martha said crossly. Yes,

the situation felt like a nightmare, but she wasn't dreaming it. It was real, and she had called her closest friend—who was inconveniently out of town—for comfort, not for denial. She said, "I already feel quite hideously detached from reality, and you'll only make it worse by telling me I'm dreaming."

Hannah's voice softened. "I'm sorry, bubbele. If you say it happened, it happened."

"It happened."

"You found a dead man."

"Yes." Not *another* dead man. Saying *another* would be inaccurate. Not as inaccurate as denial, but inaccurate all the same; the other one had been a woman, not a man. This was not a woman. (It was, more specifically, not Yolanda Young, who, unbelievably, had been threatened with death.) Once before, more than four years ago now, for what had seemed at the time to be an acceptable reason, Martha had entered an apartment uninvited. The aftermath, disturbing and ultimately dangerous, had contributed greatly to her reluctance to enter Arnold Stern's apartment. Call it foreboding, call it posttraumatic stress, call it whatever was currently fashionable, the reluctance had been acute, and she severely regretted her failure to honor it.

But she had been unwilling to make life difficult for a subordinate who was under orders. She had assured herself that such a misadventure couldn't happen to her more than once. To the police, of course; to an invading army, without a doubt. Not to a seventy-five-year-old civilian woman. Thus she had talked herself into following Rashida Grant into Arnold Stern's apartment.

The living-room windows were wide open and the room was cool. "Hello-o-o!" Rashida called again. "Anybody home?"

Still no answer.

Martha had not been in the apartment often, and not at all since Lila had moved out. The place showed no obvious signs of bachelor life; it was not only cool, it was tidy. If the missing contract was there, it should be easy to find.

It wasn't. Arnold hadn't parked it on the kitchen counter or the end tables or the dining table; he hadn't concealed it in the refrigerator or in the cupboards; it wasn't in the drawers of a sideboard that was the closest thing to a desk in the living room; it didn't lie among Lila's collection of arty ceramics in the hutch on top of the sideboard.

The master bedroom would have been the obvious next place to investigate, but its door was shut. The doors to the bathroom and the small bedroom were open, so, taking the course of least resistance, they looked next in those small spaces, Rashida Grant searching the bathroom, Martha the bedroom.

The bed had been stripped to the mattress; the dresser top was bare; all the drawers were empty. The closet door stood open; Martha saw at a glance that the closet, too, was empty.

The wall at the back of that closet, she calculated, was the one that abutted her study. It was through that wall that she had heard the thump yesterday afternoon.

They met in the hall. Rashida had found neither briefcase nor marked-up contract in the bathroom. Martha now thought that if either had spoken her mind just then, they might have retreated and advised Mr. Palladino to wait until Arnold Stern returned his call. But Rashida was under orders, so Martha shrugged and nodded, and Rashida knocked on the door of the master bedroom.

Again the only response was silence. Rashida looked at Martha. Martha sighed and nodded again. Rashida turned the knob and opened the door.

And Martha found that even to an aged female civilian, it can happen twice.

SIX

Detection

THE DETECTIVE SAT in one of the easy chairs in Martha's living room. He was named White, but he was black—well, brown—and moderately good-looking in a rangy sort of way. In an alternative universe he might have been a veteran first baseman one year away from retirement. Perhaps he had become a policeman because he couldn't hit a major league curve ball.

Huddled in on herself in the matching chair that stood at an angle to Detective White's, Martha noted that her mind was gibbering.

Arnold Stern was dead. Martha and Rashida Grant had found him—what was left of him—behind the closed door to the master bedroom. He was lying between the bed and the chest of drawers, his ruined face caked with brown dry blood. The room, in spite of wide-open windows, smelled ever so faintly of rotten meat.

They had floundered back to Martha's apartment. Rashida Grant had vomited into Martha's toilet. Clamping her tongue against the roof of her mouth and tightening all her muscles, Martha had just managed not to. She had called 911, and before long the police had come: first two uniformed patrolmen; then, in plain clothes, this Detective White and his partner, whose name Martha's memory hadn't retained; then crime-scene technicians lugging the instruments of their trade.

Detective White's partner had taken Rashida Grant somewhere else, Martha didn't know where, to hear her version, while Martha sat in her own living room in an easy chair that obliquely faced the one occupied by Detective White. Gulping tea that was nearly too hot for her tongue, she clutched at self-command, aware that it would take more than tea and deep breathing to drive the image of that destroyed face from behind her closed eyelids, and the pervasive faint smell of that bedroom from the back of her nose. A quivering in her midsection wouldn't stop.

Arnold had been shot at close range. A handgun had been lying near his right hand. Martha supposed that tests would eventually reveal whether that had been the gun that had done the damage and if so, whether it was Arnold who had pulled the trigger.

The preliminary estimate, Detective White told Martha, was that Arnold had died yesterday. Sunday. An autopsy would probably establish a more exact time of death. What had Martha been doing yesterday, he asked, and where, and with whom?

She told him. He wrote in a notebook. She went into her bedroom, rummaged in the handbag she had carried to the concert, and brought the ticket stub out to him. He looked at it, wrote in the notebook again, and handed it back. He asked if, while she was at home during the time between the concert and her visit to Yolanda Young, she had heard anything that might have been a shot.

No, she hadn't. Might that mean that the shot—or was it shots?...

One shot. It did the job.

She gulped more tea and resumed. Might the fact that she hadn't heard the shot mean that it had been fired while she was away from home? (The point seemed important, but she couldn't have said why.)

Not necessarily, he said. Given the layouts of the two apartments, she might not have heard it.

It was while she was thinking about the layouts of the apartments that she remembered the thump she had heard on the other side of her study wall. It hadn't sounded at all like a shot, she told him; it was unquestionably a thump on the wall, as if someone were moving something in the closet of the Sterns' small bedroom.

Detective White spent several minutes trying to narrow down the time when she'd heard it. The best she could do was between five and six. The vagueness irritated her more than it seemed to bother Detective White.

When had she last seen Arnold Stern?

"A couple of weeks ago," she said. "I stopped by to tell him I would be away for ten days over Memorial Day, and he said he would be out of town the weekend after that. The weekend just past."

"Do you know if he actually went?"

"I've been assuming he did, but I don't know for sure."

"Do you know where he was going?"

"Upstate to visit his daughter."

"Upstate being—?"

"A little town in the Catskills." She knew the name of the place and was annoyed that she couldn't dredge it up. "Their daughter is a resident in a school for the handicapped. She's profoundly retarded. The reason I've been taking it for granted that he went is that they've always been conscientious about visiting her."

"They?"

"Arnold and his wife."

"There is a wife? He was wearing a wedding band, but there weren't any woman's clothes in the apartment."

"She moved out a few weeks ago."

"Her name?"

"Lila."

"Where is she now?"

"Staying with a friend in Brooklyn, I believe. I don't have the name or address."

"Any children besides the daughter upstate?"

"Two. Adult. A son and a daughter."

"Do you have their addresses?"

"No. I should think they'd be somewhere in the apartment."

"How was he taking the separation? Did he seem depressed?"

"I couldn't say. I've seldom seen him since Lila left. Just now and then at the elevator. In any case,

I'm not sure I'd have noticed. He has always struck me as basically a serious man, so I don't know how obvious depression would be.''

"Do you know what led to the breakup?"

"No."

"Any rumors? Another man in her life? Another woman in his?"

Martha barely hesitated. This was a police investigation: gossip might be, or at least might lead to, evidence. "I have no direct knowledge," she said, "but I've recently heard a rumor. Less than a rumor, actually; just an innuendo." It seemed important to get that right.

"Yes?" he prompted.

"Arnold is—was—president of our co-op board, and I recently heard someone suggest that one of the female board members may have had an undue influence on his decisions."

Detective White didn't exactly smile, but the muscles around his eyes moved as if he wanted to. "Is that a roundabout way of saying they were having an affair?"

"I don't know."

"Which female board member are we talking about?"

"Yolanda Young. Please understand, what I heard wasn't even as substantial as a rumor. Just an innuendo. It could have been no more than gossipy guesswork."

"Who was doing the…innuendoing?"

"Either Nadine Jones or Bird Buckley. I don't recall which one."

"Do they live in this building?"

"Yes. I don't know which apartment." He could find out easily enough.

"Would you know if he had any enemies?"

All at once a dreadful impulse to laugh pushed at the back of Martha's throat. She suppressed it and said, "He was the president of the co-op board. The air conditioner failed during the heat wave we just had. The better question would be, 'Did he have any friends?'"

Again Detective White held back a smile. "How about—let's say—*specific* enemies?"

If he had been a first baseman, and if Martha had been eleven years old, and if she had lived in a baseball town, and if she had possessed his baseball card, she'd have asked for his autograph....

Gibbering again. She recognized it as a form of avoidance, and the realization helped her to stop. The tea and the discipline of speaking coherently helped, as well. The inner quivering had abated, and her wits were settling into their customary organized state. And this inner settling was fortunate, for saying what she was about to say demanded more inner discipline than had yet been called for.

"*Enemy* is too strong a word," she warned, "but for what it's worth, one of the shareholders was joking about shooting the board."

"Who was that?"

"Jeff Callaghan. He's been trying to sell his apartment, and the board just turned down his prospective buyer. I must emphasize that he was only blowing off steam, and I'm telling you about him only because you'll undoubtedly be hearing it from others and I don't want you to give it undue weight.''

"You know him pretty well?"

"Well enough to make that judgment, I think. In any case, a group has been formed to try to elect some new people to the board, and he's taking part in that. If we succeed, there'll be no need for shooting.''

He asked for names and wrote them down and asked if there was anything else she could tell him.

"How about an anonymous death threat?" As soon as she spoke, she cringed at her unintentionally whimsical tone.

White raised his eyebrows. "That would help, yes. Who was being threatened?"

"Yolanda Young."

He glanced down at his notebook.

"The innuendee," she confirmed. "She'd invited me down to her apartment, I'm not really sure why, and while I was there, she got a phone call that she said was a death threat.''

"She said."

"Yes."

"Could you hear the caller?" A faint emphasis on *you*.

"No. It went like this: The telephone rang. She got up from her chair and went over to it and picked it up and said, 'Hello,' and then 'Who's calling?' She didn't say anything for a few seconds; then she hung up—

slammed the phone down, actually—and then she picked it up and dialed. There was a short wait, and then she said, 'Arnold, call me,' and hung up. She looked quite disturbed. I asked what was wrong, and she said she had just received a death threat. She said the caller said she should stop messing up people's lives or she would die."

"Did you hear those words yourself?"

"No. That's what she told me."

"And then she tried to call someone named Arnold. Would that have been the victim?"

"I assumed so."

"As if she thought he was alive."

"Presumably."

He wrote rapidly. Then he looked up and asked if she had seen any strangers in the building on Sunday.

She hadn't. "But I was out for a good part of Sunday," she reminded him. "And I can't guarantee that I'd recognize everyone who lives in the building. I did exchange a few words with a nephew of one of the tenants. Peter Sanders. His aunt is Irene Xendopoulis, in apartment 2E. She was admitted to the hospital on Thursday, and he came by on Sunday to get some things for her. She's currently at Saint Vincent's."

He scribbled. "Anything else?"

"That's all I can think of."

"Okay. Thanks. Now, one more thing. Just routine. It would be a good idea to do this in the kitchen, if that's all right with you."

It was her fingerprints he was after. Just routine, he said again; they needed to eliminate her fingerprints from all the others they would find in Arnold's apartment. Having read her share of police procedurals, Martha didn't need the explanation. She led him into the kitchen, where he opened the small gym bag he was carrying and laid out on the counter a tube of printer's ink, a small square of glass, a roller, and a card with two rows of blank rectangles. She realized how tense she still was when she had trouble relaxing her fingers enough to let him roll them in the ink and on the card. But at last the process was complete. He produced a pack of Handi Wipes; she wiped most of the ink from her fingers and washed off the rest under the kitchen faucet.

After he had given her his card and she had seen him out the door and turned the dead bolt behind him, she had settled herself on the chaise and picked up the living-room phone, and that was when she put in the call to Hannah Gold, her closest friend, who was inconveniently visiting friends sixty miles up the Hudson Valley. It was Hannah whose pungent sympathy had supported Martha through her retirement and then through Edwin's final prolonged illness, and it was Hannah to whom, almost without needing to think about it, she now turned.

And Hannah exclaimed, "Martha, no, you didn't!" and Martha scolded her, because, yes, she had. And when she had persuaded Hannah that, yes, it had happened, it really had happened, Hannah said, "Hold on a minute," and for a short time Martha heard the muffled sound that a telephone makes when a hand covers the mouthpiece, and then the muffling ceased and Hannah said, "We want you to come up here."

"Hannah…"

"Don't argue. You can't be sitting there all by yourself next door to a murder scene. Come tonight. Get on a train, and we'll meet it."

"I have a job to finish."

"Cancel it."

"I can't. My client firms have deadlines."

A sigh gusted through the phone. "Deadlines were invented to put off. You just stumbled over a dead man and you're in shock. You won't admit it, but you are."

Martha opened her mouth to renew her protest, but no words came. Hannah was right: she was in shock.

"You're right," she said.

"So get out of there and get up here and let people take care of you, for a change. Tonight. Take Metro-North, and we'll meet you at the station."

Not since the months after Edwin's death had anyone really taken care of her. Not since that miserable time had she needed anyone to. "Tomorrow morning," she said.

Hannah knew when almost was enough. "All right, tomorrow," she said.

AN HOUR LATER, Martha, who seldom swore, was cursing her devotion to duty. Her head ached, and every muscle seemed to have gone slack. Her body probably needed food, but the thought of swallowing closed her throat. Bloody images kept sliding between her eyes and the screen. She longed for sleep but was afraid to relinquish control of her mind.

The telephone interrupted her distress. Grateful for the respite, she got up from her desk, went out to the living room, and sank onto the chaise to take the call.

It was Ruth Kaplowitz. "We've just heard," she said. "Are you all right?"

One's impulse is to reassure, to say, *Yes, I'm fine,* but having already admitted her non-fineness to Hannah, Martha had no trouble resisting that impulse.

"I'm rather shaken," she said.

"Would it help to come up and talk about it? Or not talk about it and just be with somebody?"

"Would it bother your boys if we talked about it?"

"They're clued in. We've had a family discussion, and now they're in their room zapping aliens."

A YELLOW PLACARD reading CRIME SCENE—DO NOT ENTER was affixed to the door of Arnold's apartment, and bands of yellow tape covered the cracks between door and frame.

THE KAPLOWITZES presented her with a comfortable chair that her tense muscles welcomed, hot coffee that her stomach advised her to decline, and high-fiber crackers that it considered and then accepted.

"That detective knew about Jeff's threats," said Simeon.

"I told him," Martha said. "I didn't use the word *threat.*"

"He did."

"I suppose he has to think like that. I told him I thought Jeff was just venting."

"So did we."

"And I told him about our conspiracy. I thought he should know that Jeff was involved in planning a bloodless coup."

"We made the point, too," said Ruth.

"It would be a more important point if we'd been in a position to unseat Arnold," said Simeon.

"He's unseated now," said Ruth. "We should lobby them to appoint Martha to fill the vacancy."

"Let it rest for the present," said Simeon. "It won't do to appear opportunistic."

"Maybe I'm being naive," said Martha, "but I can't believe Jeff would shoot Arnold after talking about it so openly."

"I'd say that, too," said Simeon, "if I didn't happen to know that he was in Arnold's apartment yesterday afternoon."

"He was?"

"Very much so," said Ruth. "I'm surprised you didn't hear him yelling."

"I was out."

"Oh, that's right, we met you coming in. Actually, that's why we were going out. I heard Jeff carrying on, and I thought it wouldn't hurt to get Melody out of the way, so I called down and invited her to go out for a play date with Tyler."

After a moment of thought, Martha asked, "Was he still yelling when you collected Melody?"

"Actually, I didn't collect her, Vanessa brought her up. But no, he wasn't. He was back at home."

"You're sure?"

"He answered the phone when I called. Is it important?"

Martha's head felt full of feathers. She rubbed her forehead and said, "Maybe, if I have the sequence of events right. You heard Jeff yelling, you called the Callaghans...."

"Not right away. The boys were watching the game, and I couldn't pry Tyler away until it was over."

"So some time passed between Jeff's yelling in Arnold's apartment and your calling the Callaghans. And when you called, Jeff answered the phone. In his own apartment. It wasn't a cell phone, was it?"

"No, their home number."

"So Jeff was already back at home before you went out with the children. And I was just coming home as you were going out."

"Where are we going with this?" asked Simeon.

"It's the timing," said Martha. "After I got home, I heard a bump on the wall that my apartment shares with Arnold's."

"A shot?" asked Ruth.

"No, it was the kind of bump one makes moving something heavy in a tight place."

"I see what you're saying," said Ruth. "Someone was moving around in Arnold's apartment after you got home, and it wasn't Jeff, because by then he was back in his own apartment."

"If he stayed there," said Simeon.

"After what we heard, can you see Arnold letting him back in once he was out?" said Ruth.

"Point taken," said Simeon. "Sounds to me as if that bump may let Jeff off the hook."

SEVEN

Escape

THE VIOLENT DEATH of a New York City high school assistant principal was, of course, newsworthy. Back at home again, Martha let her answering machine pick up and record a couple of reporters' calls. She did not return them, and by staying in all evening and snacking on what she could find in the cupboard and refrigerator—no hardship, for her appetite was still severely diminished—she avoided the camera crews outside the building. When she left for Grand Central in the morning, they were gone.

This wasn't her first train ride up the Hudson. Twice during her forty-plus years at Reilly, Whitman, she had taken the train to Albany to argue a case before the New York State Court of Appeals. On those trips, she had been largely unaware of the landscape: going up, her attention had been focused inward on her argument; returning, she had been too mentally drained to notice much of anything. This trip, she vowed, would be different.

Riding against the morning commuter rush, she had no trouble obtaining a window seat on the river side of the train. She successfully attended to *Emma* while the train cleared the abandoned tenements, housing projects, warehouses, tangled highway overpasses, and Harlem River drawbridges that clutter the northern reaches of the city. When her muscles registered a sharp turn to the right, she marked her place with a finger between the pages and turned her attention outward to the broad brown expanse of the Hudson, bounded on its far side by the angular columns of the Palisades.

She had, of course, traveled north of the city on a number of previous excursions—to hike in Fahnestock State Park, for instance, or to pick apples in Dutchess County orchards in the fall—but that had been while Edwin was still alive. They had made those trips by car, and the highways did not skirt the river. Generations before Robert Moses had dreamed of the Taconic State Parkway, railroad magnates had secured the rights of way along the river's banks.

Martha no longer had a car. She had long ago decided that, so long as subways, buses, and taxis existed, a car was an unnecessary nuisance in the city. For out-of-town trips, there were airplanes, limo services, trains, accommodating friends with Jeeps, and, in a pinch, Hertz and Avis and their competitors. But only in a pinch: driving riveted one's attention to the road, and why did one travel if not to attend to whatever was around one?

So after a few minutes she tucked the book away in her handbag and gazed out at the river and the wooded heights on its far bank, and presently the tension in her neck and shoulders began to seep away like water poured onto dry sand.

Time passed. The river narrowed and widened as the stony heights that dictated its course advanced and retreated in the eons-old pattern established by ancient tectonic stresses. The train hurtled past small, unsheltered platforms, and stopped from time to time at more substantial stations where people got off and other people got on.

About forty-five minutes into the hour-and-a-quarter trip, a nebulous sense of claustrophobia woke her from a shallow doze. Outside the train window, a high, vaguely ruined gray stone wall closed off the view of the river. The train clattered on, the wall disappeared, and a station sign slid into view.

OSSINING.

She came sharply awake as if someone had flipped a switch. She had just passed an abandoned cell block of Sing Sing prison.

The back of her neck tightened.

Jeff Callaghan.

Stocky, red-haired Jeff, muttering "Shoot them all" while his little girl slept in his arms.

But no. No, it couldn't be Jeff. Long before Martha had heard that bump on the wall, Jeff had left Arnold's apartment and gone back home. Someone had been alive and moving around in Arnold's apartment after Jeff had left. Someone who was not Jeff.

She commanded herself to drop the subject. This trip was supposed to be an escape.

OSSINING RECEDED, and now there were no more little local platforms for the train to rush through; the stations were larger and farther apart, and the train stopped at each one. She consulted her timetable, and just after the fourth of those stops, she clambered from her seat into the swaying aisle, hauled her wheeled overnight bag down from the luggage rack, and made her unsteady way down the aisle and through the door to the noisy exit platform at the end of the car. On the other side of the exit door's window, the jagged granite cliffs of railway cuts, black with soot accumulated during the age of steam, hurtled by. The cliffs gave way to woods and marshes; the woods and marshes slid by; the PHILLIPS LANDING sign at the edge of a narrow concrete platform glided into view; the train eased to a stop. The door opened, and she trundled her bag across the narrow gap between train and platform.

Beyond the platform rail, trees cloaked a steep hillside. The breeze that rustled their leaves stroked her face—real air, warm and a little damp after the air-conditioned chill of the train. The train door slid shut behind her; up front, the engine roared; the cars eased past, gathered speed, and rumbled off up the track. And there, dumpy in jeans and flapping shirttails, bustling down the platform with her arms outspread, was Hannah, and waiting beside the railing not far behind her were Paul and Nell Willard.

Martha received a hug from Hannah and more sedate greetings from Paul and Nell. Paul took Martha's bag. They crossed the tracks on a pedestrian bridge and descended to the parking lot, from which she was driven in a venerable Jeep up the village's main street, past antique shops and real estate offices, a bookstore and two pizzerias, a video-rental outlet, a travel agency and a couple of gas stations, and at last up into the tree-cloaked hills. Presently they turned off the paved two-lane highway onto a narrow, winding dirt road, then onto a narrower one, and finally onto a curving gravel driveway that dead-ended at a cedar-sided house tucked into the lower slope of a rocky, forested mini-mountain.

Escape.

PAUL WILLARD WAS a powerful, bearded teddy bear of a man. Like Hannah, he was a sculptor, but whereas Hannah, an honor graduate of the Fashion Institute of Technology and once upon a time Martha's dress-maker, had moved outward from clothing the human form to creating abstractions from fabric, Paul worked in a weightier medium. He scavenged tree limbs, some that had fallen in the forest, others from local arborists who hired him to help with particularly tricky pruning jobs, and when the wood had aged enough to be stable, trimmed them and combined them into forms that his New York dealer, more often than not, sold. His wife, Nell, an unintentionally childless earth mother, was a freelance writer of grant proposals, an occasional nee-dlewoman, and a close observer of the local govern-ment, from time to time reminding her elected repre-sentatives that stewardship of the landscape was at least as important as concern for the tax base. Hannah had met them years before when she and Paul had been members of the same cooperative gallery. They admired each other's work and enjoyed each other's company; the competitive ups and downs of their careers had only strengthened the friendship. Hannah had taken Martha to more than one of Paul's shows, and Martha had found much to like in his work, as well as in Paul himself, and in Nell. She would never be as close to them as she was to Hannah, but she felt good whenever she spent time with them.

AS SOON AS she had changed from her traveling oxfords into walking shoes and had tucked the bottoms of her pant legs into the tops of her socks to ward off ticks, they took her on an easy introductory hike along a deer path through the woods at the base of their toy mountain, to a slope covered with blossoming mountain laurel. Tomorrow they would tackle a sterner trail.

Among the head-high shrubs covered with white-and-pink blossoms that rivaled any domesticated rhododendron Martha had ever seen, they perched on lichen-grizzled boulders to eat sandwiches of homemade hummus on homemade sourdough bread. The past week's calamity retreated into the back of Martha's mind, hardly more disturbing than a half-attended-to report of colliding galaxies at the outer edge of the universe.

THEY RETURNED BY a circuitous route that led past a cedar-sided building situated behind a dense growth of heavily leafed shrubs about a hundred yards from the house. It was the size of a large shed, but with none of the crudeness implied by that word. Garage doors formed half of its front; a narrow drive that was little more than a pair of well-defined wheel tracks snaked down to the main driveway. Beside the garage doors was a little stoop and a people-sized door, from which a bark-surfaced foot trail meandered away toward the house.

"Paul's studio," said Nell.

"May I peek?" asked Martha.

"I'll send you home if you don't," said Paul. He extracted a key chain from his jeans pocket, unlocked the door, and stood aside.

The interior smelled agreeably of sawdust and pine resin. When Paul flicked the switch, a ceiling-wide array of fluorescent tubes cast shadowless light on a workbench and a table saw in the middle of the space and on shelves of tools covering one wall. An open sketchbook, its exposed sheet covered with pencil sketches, lay on the workbench, and tree limbs, some bare, some with bark still on them, were piled on the floor.

A battered sofa and a little table stood against the wall next to the door. The table held a lamp and a magazine that was folded open to show a half-page photograph that was obviously a shot of one of Paul's works; it illustrated an article entitled "Paul Willard's Continuing Mastery." The byline of the article was Everett Upton.

Everett Upton, her neighbor and fellow insurgent, the transplanted Englishman with the terrible toupee, had invaded her sanctuary. So much for escape.

She must have exhibited some discomposure, for Paul said, "You all right?"

She gathered her wits. "This reviewer. Everett Upton. Do you know him?"

"Old Ev? Sure. Do you?"

"He lives in my building."

"Is that a fact? Now somebody's supposed to say, 'Small world.' He's kind of an odd duck, but he likes my work. Do you know him well?"

"Not very. That toupee of his is rather off-putting."

Paul laughed. "I can ignore it as long as he gives me good reviews. If you care for me, please do likewise. Just don't leave him alone with the family silver."

"Paul," said Nell, "you're being very, very naughty. Martha, I should have asked before: Can you tolerate vegetarian for an entire day?"

"Gladly," said Martha.

The family silver?

SUPPER WAS meatless lasagna and green salad. It was served, with no further mention of the family silver, at a picnic table on the back deck. They lingered outside after they ate, while the sun slipped down the sky and dusk began to rise from the deeper pockets between the hills. Out of sight in the woods, a bird whistled a seven-note tune.

"What is that?" asked Martha.

"Wood thrush," said Paul.

The bird whistled again. If Nell had not banned the word, Martha would have said it sounded silvery.

"Lovely," she said instead, and wondered how it would be to live surrounded by forest, by blossoming laurel and birdsong, in a house of one's own—actually to possess walls and floors and roof, not just pieces of paper granting one the right, subject to irksome conditions, to occupy the space they enclosed, to live free of proprietary leases, bylaws, house rules, boards of directors....

As a child, she had taken it for granted that people lived in houses.

EIGHT

Lila I

BUT MARTHA NOW lived in an apartment, not a house, so when she trundled her overnight case off the elevator into the seventeenth-floor corridor late on Thursday afternoon, she was in a position to see that the police seal was gone from her next-door neighbor's door. When she approached more closely, she also observed that the door was open an inch or two.

Neighbors, whether they live in neighboring houses or neighboring apartments, look out for one another. Except, of course, when they're feuding. Martha was feuding with no one. She stopped and pressed the doorbell button. Through the crack between door and frame, she heard the four-tone chime, the faint *shush-shush* of footsteps on carpet, and the squeaky pad of rubber soles on polished floorboards. A shadow fell across the strip of foyer wall that was visible through the crack. The door opened, and Martha found herself in the presence of Lila Stern. Arnold's wife. Now his widow.

At first glance, Lila didn't look especially widowish: her shoulder-length brown hair was newly frosted with gold highlights, and her skin was matte with foundation and blusher, and although she was dressed for physical work in jeans and a blue-and-white checked shirt, the jeans had been pressed with a crease, and the shirt was scarcely rumpled. A closer look, however, revealed what the makeup couldn't entirely conceal: the pouched skin under her eyes.

"Yes?" Lila said. "Oh, Martha. Hi."

"I'm sorry if I'm intruding," Martha said. "The door was open, and I thought I'd better check."

"Oh. Oh, heavens. Thanks. I was bringing in some boxes, and I guess I didn't get it latched." Lila swung the door wider. "Come in."

For an instant, the nerves at the back of Martha's nose seemed to detect the ever-so-faint metallic odor of blood. "I don't want to interrupt anything," she said.

"You aren't," Lila said. "Not at all. Come on in. Please."

Entering that apartment was just about at the bottom of Martha's list of priorities, but Lila's invitation, although conventional in wording, was desperate in tone. Martha risked another couple of shallow breaths. This time nothing triggered a gag reflex. Memory must have deceived her nerve endings. She said, "For a minute or two," and eased her wheeled bag over the threshold.

Lila closed the door and turned the dead bolt. "Been away?" she asked.

"For a couple of days."

"Good for you. I've got an agents' tour coming up,

Paris and Rome, and I can't wait." Lila was a travel agent; some years ago Martha had learned that travel agents were regularly treated to demonstration tours in order that they might more knowledgeably sell the product to their clients. "Come on in," Lila urged. "Sit down. Don't mind the mess."

Martha went on in, and discovered that the "mess" consisted of two cartons in the middle of the living-room floor, one of them closed and sealed, the other a quarter full of newspaper-wrapped objects nestled among plastic foam peanuts, along with a pile of newspapers, a roll of brown sealing tape, and a pair of scissors. The top shelf of the hutch was nearly empty. Lila was packing her ceramics collection.

"Sorry for the mess," Lila said again. "I've got to get this place ready for viewing before I go. They told me at work they could send someone else on this trip, but all I want to do is get away and think about something else. Am I being callous?"

"You must do what feels right."

"I don't know what I feel, except that I've got to get out of here."

"I take it you won't be moving back in."

"I couldn't stand it. And I can't afford it, anyway. Sit down, please. How about some coffee?"

"Not just now, thanks."

"You're smart. Arnold only bothered with instant. Sit down. Please." Her tone still verged on desperation.

Martha settled obediently into a chair and stood her

case next to it. "Are you trying to clear out the apartment all by yourself?" she asked.

"Just packing the pots." Lila sank onto a sofa. "The movers will clear it out, and I've got one of those cleaning services coming in, the ones that do really heavy jobs. Sandy's cleaning girl—Sandy's my friend I'm staying with—her girl did this room. You wouldn't believe what a mess the police left, black fingerprint dust all over everything. The girl did a great job, but I couldn't ask her to deal with—" She tilted her head toward the back. "If that service can deal with fires and floods, I guess they can deal with what's back there. Martha, I have a huge favor to ask. Say no if it's too much. I told you, I have this trip. The cleaners may have a cancellation, so they could come before I get back. Would you possibly be willing to take the keys and let them in if it turns out they do?"

"Of course," said Martha. It was the smallest of favors.

"Oh, thank you. I'll bring you the keys when I'm done with this." Lila closed her eyes. "It seems so heartless. He's barely buried, and I'm rushing our whole life out the door." She massaged her lids with her fingertips. "I just can't get hold of what's happening. That gun. I hated that gun. I told him… He thought it would keep him safe, and look what… Martha, who did this?"

"I don't know."

"Someone hated him so much.… I can't seem to make them understand. I didn't hate him. I told him, that black detective, I told him I didn't hate Arnold; I just didn't want to live with him anymore. I didn't love him anymore—I didn't think I did—but I didn't hate him. I would never... He's the father of my children, for God's sake.''

"Yes."

"And if you want to be crass, there's no money in it.'' She opened her eyes. "That's how they think, isn't it? Who gets the do-re-mi. Well, it isn't true. I'm worse off with him dead. All I've got is my salary and what I can get for this place. If anyone will ever want it. He didn't have anything to leave except this place and his life insurance, and that goes into a trust fund for Ellen. I'm a trustee, along with our lawyer, and I can't touch any of it except to spend it for her benefit, and it isn't going to be enough to cover it all, so I'll—'' Lila broke off. "You don't want to hear all this."

Martha was neither eager nor reluctant; she already knew the basics. Ellen was the Sterns' youngest child. A disastrous delivery had left her with such severe brain damage that they had ultimately, and reluctantly, agreed to institutionalize her. The place they had chosen was outside the city. Lila and Arnold had alternated weekend visits.

Lila stood up abruptly, stepped over the pile of newspapers, and took down one of the pieces from the hutch. "You want to know why I got fed up? Look at this." She thrust it toward Martha.

Martha took the pot. It was ceramic, but that was about all it had in common with the other pieces. Lila collected modern work, colorfully glazed abstract sculptural forms. Compared with the others, this piece looked almost austere. It was terra cotta, a reddish brown saucer on a short pedestal, with a handle on each side of the bowl and a mythological black figure, a faun or a satyr, in the middle. It looked like something one might view in a glass case at the Metropolitan Museum of Art.

"It looks Greek," Martha said.

"It isn't mine," Lila said. "I never saw it before."

"Where did it come from?"

"Can't you guess?"

Martha raised her eyebrows.

"Who did he know who was Greek?"

"Irene Xendopoulis? I know they were friends."

"If you want to call it friends. He was flirting with her. It's what he did. He'd put on these acts, these different personae, like one of those monologuists, playing different parts? For her, it was archaeology. They'd sit around talking about digs and artifacts and how he *wished*—" her voice slid up the scale into parody "—he *wished* he could go on digs, but he couldn't spare the time because he had to teach summer school to pay for Ellen's school."

That was flirting? It sounded to Martha like a friendly discussion of a common interest.

"He made it sound all brave and heroic," Lila said, "and I guess it was convincing, but it was just an act. He wasn't a frustrated archaeologist. He took exactly three credits of archaeology in his life, and that wasn't because he was hot for scratching around in the dirt;

it was because it was a required course for history majors. He went on exactly one dig in his life, back when he was at City College, one day at some Indian encampment upstate, and that was a course assignment. But he just couldn't resist making a play for attention. A woman's attention. I honestly think that's what finally sent me out the door. I just couldn't take the…the fakery anymore.''

Lila had to be exaggerating. Martha, who was undeniably a woman, would surely have noticed if Arnold Stern had made a play for her attention. He had been neighborly, yes, but flirting? Never.

This was not to say, though, that Lila might not have the essentials right. Perhaps, Martha thought, she was too old to be flirted with. Irene Xendopoulis was (as Martha's middle-western mother might have said) no spring chicken, but she was at least ten years younger than Martha. And single. Perhaps Martha had been too married. But she had noticed no change in Arnold's manner after she was widowed.

Or perhaps Arnold actually had made a play for her attention and she had been so old, and so married, even after Edwin died, that she had mistaken his behavior for simple neighborliness.

She looked down at the pot in her hands. ''This had better be brought to the attention of the police,'' she said.

''You think?''

''I do.''

''You think it's a—'' again Lila's voice slid into parody ''—a *clue?*''

Martha wondered if the word was much in use in the NYPD. "It's an anomaly, at least," she said. "Do you have Detective White's number?"

"At Sandy's."

"I have his card at home." Martha pushed herself out of the chair. "I'll get it. Or you can come with me and use my phone."

"No."

"Lila…"

"I'm sorry, that was rude. I don't mean to be rude. It's just that I've got to get out of here before I lose my mind, and with the cleaners maybe coming while I'm gone, I've got to get my pots packed before I go. I'll call him as soon as I get back to Sandy's."

"Yes, you must. In the meantime, I don't think you should leave it here, with nobody in the apartment. It's probably quite valuable."

"It's been okay so far."

"But the police seal isn't on the door anymore."

"Oh. Well, I guess you're right, but I don't know what I'd do with it. I can't take it to Sandy's. We've got the two of us bumping into each other in her tiny little studio, and she has a cat."

"What are you doing with your own pots?"

"Leaving them here for the movers. Look, why don't you take it?"

On the verge of demurring, Martha reconsidered. The suggestion wasn't altogether outrageous. She lived alone and petless in a space designed for three. There was little risk that she would knock the thing over by accident.

"Just for now," Lila urged. "Until I can figure out what to do with it." She closed her eyes again. "I know it's an awful lot to ask, but I'm just overwhelmed."

CONSEQUENTLY, when Martha at last maneuvered her bag into her own apartment with one hand, she was cradling in her other hand that fragile, probably Greek, presumably expensive, and possibly significant anomaly, now abundantly wrapped in newspaper.

She parked the bag in the bedroom, carried the pot into her study, opened the closet door, and gazed dubiously at the miscellany of office supplies piled on the shelf and the out-of-season clothes hanging from the rod. She closed the door and carried the pot back to the living room.

Martha did not consider herself a collector, but she did own two small sculptures, which she displayed on a small table in a corner of the living room. One of the little pieces was a Hannah Gold fabric construction that she had bought years ago, partly because Hannah was a friend but mainly because she enjoyed looking at it. Hannah's dealer assured her that the piece had quadrupled in value as Hannah's reputation had grown, but nothing short of imminent starvation would ever induce her to sell it. The other piece—a sort of cat's cradle constructed of soldered heavy wire—was the work of another sculptor, one whom she knew less well but well enough. Her reasons for buying it had also been mixed; the purchase celebrated the end of a trying time, and she liked the piece for itself.

She moved the two pieces a few inches farther apart, freed the probably Greek pot from its wrap, and set it on the table between them. Then she went into the kitchen, put the kettle on for tea, and pondered the question of the day.

How had this anomalous pot got in among Lila Stern's ceramics?

More than likely it was Irene's; the association of (probably) ancient Greek pot with (undeniably) Greek-American archaeologist made the assumption more than merely plausible.

So why had it been in the Sterns' apartment?

The person to ask, of course, was Irene.

Maybe by now Irene was out of the ICU and accessible. Martha went back out to the living room, ready to spell *Xendopoulis* once more, but she pulled her hand back before she picked up the telephone. Any conversation that involved Arnold, Arnold's widow, or the contents of Arnold's apartment was apt to involve Arnold's death. Martha had no way of knowing whether Irene had yet been told that Arnold was dead. Her doctor might have judged that inflicting that shock on her already stressed system would be medically unwise. And if Irene didn't know, Martha was certainly not going to be the person to spring it on her.

Detective White was the proper person to deal with this anomaly.

This train of thought, she realized, also served her own purposes. She simply didn't want to be required to think any more about Arnold Stern's sudden and violent death. Talking about it or consciously avoiding talking about it would be equally likely to further fray the tattered remnants of that sense of escape to which, with a sort of discouraged passion, she had been clinging since she had stepped onto the city-bound train at the Phillips Landing station.

It was Lila who must talk about this pot, and it was Detective White to whom Lila must talk about it. Detective White would, of course, talk about it to Martha, but responding to questions from the police would be considerably less stressful than breaking the news of Arnold Stern's death—or avoiding breaking it—to Irene.

The kettle whistled. She went back to the kitchen and made her tea. It wasn't until she carried it out to the living room and prepared to settle on the chaise that she noticed that the answering machine was blinking.

NINE

Lila II

SHE SAT DOWN on the chaise and pressed play. A
woman's voice said, "It's Karen Higgins. Could you
call me, please, when it's convenient?"

Karen Higgins. One of the insurgents, the one who
claimed that a "woman of color" might not be the
strongest candidate for a seat on the board.

But since Karen Higgins had volunteered to help
with the campaign, and since *now* was, in fact, convenient, Martha returned the call. Not, however, from
the phone beside the chaise; two days of escape, which
had involved a good deal of tramping up and down
over protruding roots and loose stones, followed by
this afternoon's hour and a quarter on the ill-formed
seats of Metro-North, had indeed refreshed her mind
but had left her joints demanding full horizontality.
She levered herself upright from the chaise, hobbled
wearily into the bedroom, and sat on the edge of the
bed. Prepared for phone tag, she punched in the number that Karen Higgins had recited. While the ringing
tone buzzed in her ear, she eased herself back, lifted
her legs onto the bed, and lay down full length.

Aah.

She was not subjected to phone tag. After two ringing tones, the voice that had left the message said, "Karen Higgins speaking." Martha identified herself; they exchanged a few mandatory banalities; and then a change in the timbre of Karen's voice signaled that she was introducing the real subject of the call.

Ruth Kaplowitz had told her that Martha had agreed to run for the board. But now there was a vacancy, which the board was responsible for filling. "So," said Karen, "wouldn't it be a good idea to lobby them to appoint you now? Or do you think that sounds too much like dancing on his grave?"

Martha uttered her all-purpose noncommittal *Mm.*

"Or is this too soon to hit you with it? I mean, you were the one who found him. It must have been bad."

Martha wouldn't have pegged Karen Higgins as a sensation-seeker, so perhaps this expression of sympathy was genuine. "It was bad," she said. "It still is."

"I'm sorry, I shouldn't be bothering you about it. You know, I was thinking, if his wife hadn't just gone off on one of her trips, she'd have been the one to find him instead of you."

Or if, all those years ago, the Sterns had put some other neighbor's name on their emergency-notification form.

"I guess it wouldn't have been any better for her, though," said Karen.

It wouldn't have been any better for anyone. But Karen had a fact wrong, and for some reason it seemed important to get it right. "Lila was away," Martha said, "but not on a trip."

"What do you mean?"

"She doesn't live here anymore."

"Really? They split? I didn't know that. When did it happen?"

"Two or three months ago."

"I never heard. Is that what Jeff meant about Arnold selling the apartment?"

"I presume so."

"I didn't know. I saw her leaving with a suitcase, and I thought she was just off on one of her trips."

A flicker of disquiet brought Martha upright. She stuffed a pillow between her back and the headboard and said, "When was that?"

"When was what?"

"When you saw her."

"The other day."

"Do you remember what day?"

"I think it was Sunday. Yes, it was. Sunday."

"Which Sunday?"

"This past Sunday. The—whatever—the tenth."

"You're sure?"

"I'm positive. I was coming away from a rally uptown. I was coming up the street from the R train, and she was coming down the plaza steps and getting in a taxi. She had a suitcase, and I just figured she was off on one of her trips. I didn't know they split."

Martha said, "Last Sunday."

"Right." Then, "Oh."

"Just so. Did you tell the police you'd seen her?"

"I never thought of it. The detective was asking about that meeting up at Ruth's. You know, Jeff talking about shooting the board, and Simeon saying Arnold had that gun. I never even thought about seeing her."

"You're sure it was Lila you saw?"

"Oh, yes. I used her agency to go to Aruba last winter. I swear to God, I didn't remember until just this minute. He wanted to know if I saw any strangers around the building that day, and she isn't a stranger."

"You need to tell him."

"But he must know. They must have asked the doorman who was coming and going that day."

"It was the new doorman. He may not know who Lila is."

"Oh."

"It's up to you."

"Oh, lordy. Rat on a neighbor?"

"A neighbor is dead." The doorbell *ding-donged*. Martha said, "Tell the police," and ended the call.

IT WAS LILA AT the door. She was jingling a ring of keys nervously in one hand. "You don't know what a help this is," she said. "I've got to catch a plane for Paris in the morning, and this makes one less thing…"

It was impossible to pretend that Karen's call hadn't happened. Martha said, "Lila," and then thought that she must have sounded as austere as she felt, for Lila broke off and stared at her.

"Come in," Martha said. The sound of her own

voice told her that the words were a command, not an invitation. She stepped back.

Lila hesitated for a moment; then she stepped into the foyer. "What?" she said.

Martha closed the door. "Do the police know you were here last Sunday?" she asked.

"What do you mean?"

"You were here that Sunday."

"Here?" Lila looked around the foyer.

The action struck Martha as theatrical. "In the building," she said.

Lila shook her head. "No."

"Yes," said Martha. "You were seen."

"It couldn't—who says I was here?"

"Someone in the street."

"Oh, God." Lila's face seemed to crumple. "I didn't know anyone…"

Martha waited.

Lila drew an audible breath. "Yes," she said, "yes, I was here. But I didn't…I never even saw him."

"Saw whom?"

"Arnold. Honestly, I never saw him. I just came to get my summer clothes. It was so hot, I needed them all week, but I didn't want to see Arnold, so I bought a couple of blouses and waited for the weekend. It was his weekend to visit Ellen, so I knew he wouldn't be here on Sunday. And he wasn't. Not as far as I knew, he wasn't. I never saw him. I just got my clothes and left."

"Have you told the police?"

"I didn't think anyone knew."

"The police told you your husband was shot dead, and you didn't tell them you were here on the day it happened."

Lila shook her head again. "I was afraid to. They told me someone shot him, and I was afraid to say I was here. I know what they think, about husbands and wives. I didn't think anyone knew. The doorman's new, he came after I left, so he didn't know who I was, and I didn't see anyone I knew."

"You were here on the afternoon your husband was killed, and you didn't tell the police. You withheld information pertinent to a homicide investigation. That is called hindering prosecution, and it's a criminal offense."

"I didn't." Lila's voice rose. "I didn't hinder anything. There wasn't anything I could tell them. So help me God, I never saw Arnold. And I never, ever in my entire life touched that horrible gun. Not even when I lived here. Not once."

"Did you go into the master bedroom Sunday?"

"No, I did not. The door was closed, and trust me, I didn't have any desire to pay a visit to—what do they call it—the marital chamber. My clothes were in the little room, in the closet, and I just went straight back there and packed them up and went out again. I never saw Arnold. Alive or—" She caught her breath. "—alive or dead."

It might be the truth. "What time were you here?"

"Five-ish. Maybe later. I had a thing to go to, and I came here after. I was afraid I might be pushing it, coming that late, but he usually stopped to eat on the way home and didn't get home until later. I didn't see him, I swear I didn't see him. I didn't see anyone.''

"How did you get past the doorman?''

"I jingled my keys at him like I belonged here, and he didn't say anything.''

Keys? Martha remembered something that had puzzled her. ''Was the police lock on when you came up here?'' she asked. Her voice was still converting questions into demands.

"No, it wasn't.'' Paradoxically, Martha's anger seemed to have restored some of Lila's balance. ''Why?''

"You're sure?''

"Yes, I'm sure. The police lock was not on, and I was afraid that meant Arnold was home. But then I thought, well, so what if he is? It's still my place. I still have a right to go there.''

"Did you lock it when you left?''

"No. I thought there must be some reason he left it unlocked.'' Lila looked at her watch. ''If you're done making accusations, I've got to get back to Sandy's. I've got a million things to do before I leave tomorrow.'' She dangled the key chain from a finger. ''Still want to help me out?''

Neighbors were still neighbors. ''Yes, of course,'' Martha said, and took the keys.

THE STORY WAS plausible. It could even be true. Lila's demeanor could have persuaded the doorman that she was a legitimate resident. And it must have been Lila, packing her summer clothes in the small bedroom, who had bumped the wall.

And if Lila was telling the truth about the master bedroom door—if she had found it closed, and left it closed—then when Martha heard the bump, Arnold could already have been lying dead behind that door in the master bedroom.

And that meant that the bump told one nothing about Jeff Callaghan's guilt or innocence. Jeff could have shot Arnold and left him behind the closed bedroom door and gone home before Lila ever got there and bumped the wall; Arnold could have been lying dead in the master bedroom all the time Lila was there collecting her summer clothes.

The quiver had returned to Martha's midsection. She didn't want to know all this. She should have stayed up in the hills for a week. A month. A year. Perhaps for the rest of her life. But that option wasn't open; she was here, and she knew what she knew.

But sorting through these appalling *coulds* and *maybes* was Detective White's job, not hers. The thought brought her a small degree of comfort. She found his card and picked up the telephone. But then she put it down again. Karen Higgins and Lila Stern knew what she knew, and their knowledge was firsthand. Let them take a little responsibility for a change.

TEN

Village

MARTHA TOOK two aspirin and went to bed, where residual weariness from her exertions in the hills overrode her concern about unannounced visitors to Arnold's apartment and bumps on the wall and allowed her to enjoy a reasonably restful night. In the morning, a half-century of habit sent her to her computer. In spite of the temperature, which was rising again, and the air conditioner, which was all too evidently not yet repaired, work was an escape almost as potent as travel.

An hour later she modified the thought: work was an escape for the mind, but the body had other needs. Her stressed and aging knees, forced to remain inactive under her desk, were letting her know that this professional diligence was doing them no good at all.

By midafternoon, it was clear that she needed to go out. A little mild walking on the level often eased those bothersome knees of hers, and the heat might be more tolerable outdoors. She shut down the computer, went out, and followed a familiar route, west and a little south, to Washington Square Park.

The square, of course, was not the Hudson Highlands, but the rustling green ceiling of leafed-out trees
provided cooler shade than that cast by the hard sur-
faces of the city, and offered some escape from disa-
greeable ruminations, as well, if one concentrated on
attending to the world around one. This being New
York City, much was going on. At the concrete game
tables, chess players pondered their moves; in fenced
enclosures, dogs chased Frisbees; on the benches,
readers read and lovers embraced; sunbathers basked
on the rim of the fountain; and on the concrete walks,
in-line skaters swerved on whispering plastic wheels
around those who, like Martha, simply walked.

What, she suddenly wondered, had become of those
clattery old steel clamp-on roller skates of her childhood? And her skate key, where might that have got
to? Rusted to dust in some middle-western landfill, no
doubt. How she had loved roller-skating, the long,
steady swoops, le-e-e-ft, ri-i-i-ght, speeding along the
quiet summer-afternoon sidewalks on fantasized mis-
sions, carrying some imagined Message to some shadowy Garcia. She had never really taken to roller rinks;
the arm-in-arm indoor circling was a serviceable
courtship device, but as entertainment, it was an in-
adequate substitute for swooping along those endless
strips of concrete under the high middle-western sky.
In those days, knees were a concern only when one
fell and skinned them.

Eventually she turned toward home. It wasn't until
she passed a Sabrett vendor and a Good Humor cart
on the perimeter of the park that she realized that she

had worked through lunchtime. Hot dogs didn't attract her, but ice cream was tempting. Not, however, a Good Humor bar. Her roller-skating reverie had ripened into a comprehensive nostalgia; what she wanted was a childhood treat that predated Good Humor bars. What she wanted was the messy richness of an ice-cream cone.

A couple of blocks beyond her building, near the R train stop on Broadway, was a Häagen-Dazs shop. She passed the sidewalk vendors and headed north and east.

THE ICE-CREAM SHOPS of Martha's childhood had offered vanilla, chocolate, and strawberry. She had always chosen chocolate: her tongue declared that strawberry ice cream did not taste a bit like strawberries, and why bother with ice cream at all if all you were going to have was vanilla? Now she was confronted with a range of choices that approached infinity—chocolate chocolate chip, vanilla Swiss almond, cherry vanilla, rum raisin, butter pecan, pistachio....

Some of what is called progress really is progress. She ordered butter pecan and pulled four napkins from the dispenser.

As she was leaving the shop, she found that Greenwich Village, as from time to time it will do, was behaving like the village it claimed to be. That is to say, she met neighbors on the street. Vanessa Callaghan, in a tank top and a brilliantly flowered ankle-length skirt, was escorting Melody and Tyler Kaplowitz, both of them in shorts and T-shirts, to the ice-cream shop.

Having only recently realized that the bump on the wall did not, after all, clear Jeff Callaghan of suspicion, Martha was not eager for a neighborly chat with Jeff Callaghan's wife. But this was a village, and civility must be preserved, so when Vanessa paused, converted her habitual pout into a wavery smile, and said, "Well, hi there," Martha paused, as well, produced what she hoped was a neighborly smile, and said, "Hello."

Melody, however, wanted no more of neighborliness than Martha did. She exclaimed, "Mommy!" and grabbed Vanessa's arm.

"Manners, Melody!" said Vanessa. "Ms. Patterson said hello."

Melody barely glanced at Martha. She muttered, "Hello," and tugged at Vanessa's arm again. "Mommy, can we get it ourself?"

Vanessa sighed and directed an apologetic moue at Martha before once more addressing her daughter. "*May* we," she instructed, "get it our*selves.*"

Melody made a face of her own. "*May* we," she mimicked accurately, "get it *ourselves?*"

Another sigh. "Magic word?"

Melody mimicked the sigh. *"Please?"*

"That's better." Vanessa rummaged in her handbag, pulled bills from her wallet, and handed them to Melody. "Bring back the change," she called as the children vanished into the shop.

Melting ice cream from her own cone dribbled onto

Martha's fingers. It distracted her from her intention to utter a parting remark and go on her way; while she was scrubbing with her handful of paper napkins, Vanessa sighed again and said, "Ruth will kill me."

The napkins matted into useless fuzz; Martha's fingers remained sticky. Licking them would be a reasonably satisfactory stopgap until she could reach soap and water, but she deemed that solution to be too indecorous for an elderly professional woman on a public sidewalk. She compressed the napkin shreds and scrubbed some more.

Vanessa was oblivious to dribble and scrub. "But everything's so awful, I just don't have the heart to say no," she continued. "I mean, what's a little thing like ice cream before dinner when—" she dropped her voice "—you know."

Martha knew. Of course she knew. This was a village; sudden and violent death had occurred; the subject was not to be avoided. "Arnold," she said.

Vanessa glanced at the ice-cream shop's door and lowered her voice further. "We don't talk about it in front of her, but she knows." Her left eyelid twitched. "The police came."

Martha's ice cream continued to melt. In the context of sudden and violent death, licking ice cream from a cone seemed as indecorous as licking her fingers, but her inner child, that mythical but powerful artifact of the psychotherapeutic profession, was unconcerned with decorum; she had been deprived of roller skates and wasn't going to lose her ice cream as well. Audible only to Martha's inner ear, this relentless creature announced *I was here first, and I want my ice cream.*

Martha obediently ran her tongue around the perimeter of the liquefying ice cream at the top edge of the cone.

Vanessa paid no attention to the indecorum. "Jeff was in Arnold's apartment that afternoon," she said. "Maybe you heard him?"

"I was out." Martha's tongue pursued another dribble. At the same time, under her feet, the sidewalk began to vibrate. She was not alarmed; the source of the disturbance was neither earthquake nor inner disquiet; it was the subway. Some fifteen feet from where she was slurping her ice cream, a flight of steps plunged down from the sidewalk to the subway platform, and down there, a train was approaching the station.

Still oblivious, Vanessa said, "Ruth told the cops she heard him yelling. I guess she felt she had to, but, well, you know what I mean. She wasn't there. She didn't know what was really going on. I mean, Jeff was up there, but all it was, he just went up to ask what we had to do to get our buyers approved. That's all, but he got, you know, a little excited. You know how he can be." Her eyelid twitched again. "Arnold was fine when he left."

Below ground, a clattering rumble peaked. Wheels squealing on rails nearly drowned it out. Compressed air, released from the brakes, hissed. Up at street level, the children emerged from the shop with their cones. Martha pushed the remaining ice cream down with her tongue and crunched the top of the cone between her teeth.

Detraining passengers came swarming up the subway stairs. The children, experienced in the ways of the city, moved out of the way and positioned themselves next to the railing that protected pedestrians on the sidewalk from tumbling into the stairwell. Licking their cones with no concern for decorum or the risk of dribbling on the heads of those who were coming up, they peered down through the iron uprights that supported the railing.

Tyler pretended to shake the uprights with his free hand. "You're *bad,* and you're in *jail!*" he yelled at Melody.

"Stop it!" shrieked Melody.

"Kids!" shouted Vanessa.

Now thought Martha. She shoved the rest of her cone into her mouth and crunched it into a swallowable mass. But as she was gulping it down to clear the way for *nice-to-have-met-you* noises, her escape was once more forestalled. Everett Upton detached himself from the tag end of the detraining crowd and uttered a British-inflected "Good afternoon, ladies. Lovely day."

Once more Martha marshaled neighborliness and responded with "Good afternoon," but even as she spoke, she found herself wondering yet again why the man persisted in wearing that absurd toupee. Baldness was an appropriate characteristic in a middle-aged man. Her own father, a man of high distinction in the state of Nebraska, had been bald.

This unneighborly musing was interrupted by a cry of "Mommy!" Leaving Tyler standing beside the subway railing and giving Everett a wide berth, Melody scuttled over to Vanessa, grabbed at her mother's arm with the hand that wasn't holding her cone, and announced, "Mommy, I have to go! Bad!"

No parent ignores such a declaration. So it was Vanessa, after all, who made the *excuse-me-glad-we-met* noises. She collected Tyler and went off at a good clip, leaving Martha and Everett standing on the sidewalk.

Conversation was called for. Martha nearly opened it by remarking that she had just seen Everett's review of Paul Willard's exhibition, but a second thought stayed her tongue. Paul's cryptic allusion to keeping Everett away from the family silver, and Nell's immediate reprimand, raised the suspicion that, in spite of Everett's favorable professional judgment of Paul's work, on a personal level the men were not on good terms.

She swerved abruptly onto a new course. "I'm glad we've met," she said. "What news do you have of Irene?"

Everett sighed. "Not the best, I'm afraid."

"Is she still in intensive care?"

"She was scheduled to be moved to the ward today, if all went well. But I'm afraid she's still not in the best of trim." He sighed again. "I do hope it does go well. She must have been quite lonely. The ICU admits no visitors except family. It's a shame, actually; her relations are rather thin on the ground, and I'm sure she feels closer to me, for instance, than she does to Peter.''

"Is he her only relative?''

"All she has left. Parents long gone, of course. There was a brother, but he died some years ago, and they weren't on the best of terms at the end.''

Martha had mediated more than a few family disagreements during her career as a trusts and estates lawyer. "Not pleasant,'' she said.

"Not pleasant at all. And it all seems quite trivial from the outside, don't you know? Her brother changed his name when he came of age, from Damon Xendopoulis to David Sanders, and his fancy created no end of trouble. Their father disinherited him. Their mother was dead, so Irene got it all and her brother got none.''

"That seems like rather an extreme reaction.''

"I should have thought so. But that's the view from the outside, of course. I understand there was a profitable import business. Irene had no interest in running it; archaeology was her heart and soul, so she sold the business and invested the proceeds.''

"She appears to live fairly comfortably.''

"Financially, yes, she does well enough. The investments were good ones, I believe, and I understand there's an adequate pension. But professionally she's miserable. Her health is too fragile to let her go on digs, and that's what she'd rather do than anything else in the world. That's the basis of our friendship, you know. I have enough acquaintance with antiquities to hold up my end of our conversations." He sighed. "I should miss those conversations badly."

"I hope it won't come to that," said Martha. "Do you know if anyone has told her about Arnold Stern's death?"

"I very much hope not. I shouldn't think it's the kind of shock her doctor would look kindly upon."

"I know they were on good terms."

"Well, yes, they were," Everett said. "Arnold was quite the expert at being on good terms with women."

ELEVEN

The Kylix

IT WAS TRUE that asking Irene about that anomalous pot would almost certainly lead to talking about Arnold; therefore, Irene shouldn't be asked. But that prohibition didn't rule out looking for other sources of information, and as they were mounting the shallow steps to the plaza beside their building, it occurred to Martha that a prime source was right at her elbow.

The lobby temperature varied no more than a degree or two from the outdoor temperature, but Boris, who must have just come on duty, had reverted to form; he was wearing his jacket.

When they were out of earshot behind the bronze screen, Martha pressed the elevator's call button and said, "I have a question for you. Lila Stern was collecting some of her things from the apartment yesterday, and she came across a piece of pottery that isn't hers. It looks Greek, so she thought it might have some connection with Irene, but we can't think why it would have been in the Sterns' apartment. I don't believe it would be wise to bother Irene about it just now—it might lead into forbidden territory...." She glanced inquiringly at Everett.

"A-a-ah, yes," he said. "Most unwise."

"But since you're a friend of hers," Martha continued, "and it's within your area of expertise, I wonder if by any chance you know anything about it."

He was silent for a moment. Then he said, "Sorry, I'm trying to think. Could you describe it?"

She described it, augmenting words with gestures.

"A-a-ah, yes," he said. "A kylix. Yes, she does have one. Quite a nice piece, actually. I believe I mentioned it in an article at one time. A very nice piece."

"Would you know it if you saw it?"

"Oh, yes, I think so. Yes, I'm quite sure I should."

The elevator arrived. It was not the one Everett would normally take; he lived in the other wing of the building; but the tale of the pot had evidently captured his attention, for he made no move to head off to the other elevator.

Martha pressed her finger on the call button again and left it there to hold the elevator open in front of them. "Then I wonder," she said, "if you would be willing to come up to my place and take a look at it."

She sensed the slightest of hesitations. A late arrival, she supposed, would distress Everett's perpetually ailing wife. "Only if you have the time," she added. "I've taken charge of it temporarily, and I'd be more comfortable if I knew where it belongs, but it isn't urgent."

But Everett squared his shoulders, which had

slumped slightly, and said, "Not at all. Now will do very well. Yes, very well. I'm curious myself."

She released the call button, and they stepped inside.

EVERETT TURNED the pot from side to side, studied it top and bottom, and finally cradled it in his hands. "Oh, yes," he said. "Yes, indeed."

"It's Irene's?"

"It's hers. Marvelous little thing, isn't it?" His fingertips caressed the black figure in the center of the bowl.

"It's the real thing?"

"Oh, indeed. A kylix, with satyr. A wine cup. Can you imagine sipping your retsina from this every day?"

"How do you suppose it got in among Lila's ceramics? She collects contemporary work."

"Haven't the foggiest." His fingers stroked the outer curve of the bowl.

"Lila thought Irene might have given it to Arnold."

"Oh, I scarcely—" Everett broke off and drew in his lower lip. He released it and said, "It's worth, I'd say, two or three thousand. The higher figure if it comes with provenance."

"Goodness."

"Yes. A bit dear for a friendly gift, one would think. Still, I suppose it's possible. Arnold did have that knack."

"Is it a souvenir of one of her digs?"

"Oh, no. Not at all." He set it carefully back on

the table between Martha's two very different little sculptures. "Irene is a thorough professional. What is important to her is not the *ding an sich,* the object in itself, you know, but the object *in situ*—in relation to where it is and to the other artifacts that accompany it. The full historical record. For Irene, the object divorced from its context, however lovely it may be in and of itself, is of only minor interest."

"But she had this piece."

"That was by way of being an accident."

"How on earth does one acquire a two-thousand-dollar antique Greek pot by accident?"

"Well, I don't think she'd mind my telling you. It was a gift from an old lover."

"Presumably an affluent old lover."

"One supposes so. It seems he never properly understood her work. He knew she was of Greek descent—one could hardly fail to be aware of that—and he knew she dug up ancient pots for a living, so it seems he thought an ancient Greek pot that had already been dug up would be an appropriate token of his affection. That, she said, was on the occasion of her forty-fifth birthday. I understand the relationship was terminated well before she turned forty-six."

"But she kept the pot."

"Oh, yes. I suppose she thought that since it was already hopelessly out of context, she might as well have it as anyone else. She knows its monetary value."

"So we're back to where we started. Unless we suppose that she gave it to Arnold, which, as you pointed out, isn't especially plausible, how did it get in among Lila's ceramics?''

Everett stood gazing down at it and rubbing his chin. ''Well,'' he said after a moment, ''I do have one thought. When she began feeling ill—more ill than usual, that is to say—I suppose she might have asked Arnold to look after it for her. In case, you know, she had to go into hospital and leave the apartment empty.''

''Even though she didn't particularly value it?''

''Oh, as I said, she's aware of its monetary value. And I suppose there may be a bit of nostalgia for the love of yesteryear. But really, I'm only guessing. I simply don't know how it got from her place to his.''

As soon as Everett left, Martha washed her hands. She had refrained from handling the pot while her fingers retained the last gummy traces of ice cream. It was time to accept the responsibility she had wanted to avoid. She went into the living room, sat down on the chaise, and punched in Detective White's number.

Detective White was at his desk, not out pursuing malefactors. In as few words as possible, she told him about Lila's surreptitious Sunday visit and about the mysterious appearance of the kylix.

Interesting, he said. He would come right over.

He came. He listened. He put on thin cotton gloves to examine the pot and then to pack it away in a padded box. He took off the gloves to write a receipt.

"And while I'm talking to you," he said, "do you happen to know where Yolanda Young might be?

"She isn't at work?"

"Or at home, as far as we can tell. She left a voice mail at her business Tuesday night, saying she'd been called out of town. She didn't say where."

"Tuesday was the day we found Arnold."

"Yes. I was hoping you picked up something when you had that talk with her."

"Nothing. I assume you can trace the number she called from."

"Her cell phone."

Which could be anywhere. Which could, in fact, be used by anyone. "Are they sure it was her voice?" she asked.

"It was breaking up some, but her secretary thinks so."

"Thinks?"

His *Mm-hm* was a verbal shrug.

"I suppose you've tried knocking on her door."

"Yes, we have tried that." An edge in his voice advised her not to question his competence.

She didn't ask if they had tried phoning Yolanda's apartment. They would have. She did risk saying, "The doormen?"

"The night man says she didn't go out while he was on duty and the day man can't remember when was the last time he saw her leaving with the morning crowd."

If Boris said Yolanda Young hadn't gone out during

his shift, Yolanda Young hadn't gone out during his shift.

"You're sure you didn't pick up something when you were with her?" White persisted. "After she got that anonymous call, maybe?"

"Quite sure," Martha said. "I'd help if I could. With one exception. If you're planning to enter her apartment to look for her, I will not be going with you."

TWELVE

Irene

MARTHA SELDOM TRIED to sleep in the daytime—naps invariably left her feeling groggy and grouchy—but Detective White's visit, loaded on top of the emotional stress of fighting off free-floating suspicions and the physical demands of her country exertions and today's little hike in her own urban village, had left her with an energy deficit. Her eyes were refusing to stay open. She gave in and took to her bed.

She felt as if she had barely dropped off when the telephone woke her, but the bedside clock asserted that three-quarters of an hour had passed. She lifted the handset in time to cut off the third ring and, doing her best to keep her voice civil, said, "Martha Patterson speaking."

"Irene Xendopoulis, barely speaking," wheezed a familiar voice.

"They've let you out of the ICU."

"What a process." Pause for a rattly cough. "A detective was just here."

"He's been to see you already? That was fast."

"It isn't far for guys with sirens. Arnold's dead."

It was a statement, not a question. "Yes."

"Shot. With his own gun."

"That's my information."

"How stupid can a man be? I told him it was dangerous, but would he listen?" Another wheezy breath. "It's awful. I don't have so many friends that I can afford to lose one. Was it someone who hates the board?"

"That's one theory."

"Is it yours?"

"I have no theory."

"How about that wife of his?"

Hadn't Martha had enough of Lila Stern? "Why would Lila want him dead?" she asked.

"They were married."

"People can be married without wishing each other dead."

"Show me some."

"Me."

"You've forgotten. Martha, I've never liked that woman. She was jealous of everything Arnold cared about." Another noisy breath. "Why is that detective making a fuss over my kylix?"

Still groggy, and irritated by Irene's cynical dismissal of half a century of affection and trust, Martha took a moment to adjust to the sudden change of subject. "Didn't he tell you?" she stalled.

"I want to hear it from you."

"Lila Stern found your kylix keeping company with her ceramic collection, and nobody knows how it got from your place to the Sterns'."

"That's what he said."

"And you said—?"

"I said I asked Arnold to keep it when my breathing got so bad. I didn't want to leave it in my place if they were going to haul me off to the hospital. It's worth thousands." Another couple of labored breaths. "God knows what'll happen to it now."

"I should think the police will return it to you when the case is resolved."

"Arnold, a case?" A phlegmy cough. "He'd hate that."

"Probably."

"Is it going to get resolved?"

"I have no idea."

"Is fussing about my little pot going to resolve it?"

"Your little pot is a loose end. They have to see if it's tied to anything important. Did you tell Detective White you want it back?"

"I don't know what I'd do with it."

"What you've always done with it, I should think."

"Can't. My beastly doctor's telling me I have to move. Some bosh about assisted living, or whatever they call the stupid business."

"Oh, dear."

"Wrong. The words are *Damn this shitty business to hell and back.*"

"Just so."

"He's telling me I can't live on my own. I've been on my own since I was eighteen. Not that I did much of a job of it. It isn't like we didn't know. Coffin nails. Remember that? We called them coffin nails. We knew. So now I'm a helpless old crock who has to have a keeper, and the social worker is shoving names and addresses at me, and I don't know enough about the business to pick one that won't kill me. Do you know anything about this racket?''

"Not in any organized way. If you'd like, there's someone I can call.''

"I'd like.''

MARTHA HAD TAKEN Irene's call lying on her bed. Now she struggled reluctantly to her feet, fetched her Rolodex card file from her study, carried it out to the phone in the living room, arranged herself comfortably on the chaise, and punched in the number for the Association for the Elderly and Retired. She had met Sunny Searle, the executive director of that organization, several years ago during her brief stint as a pro bono attorney at West Brooklyn Legal Services, and since leaving West Brooklyn, had from time to time done some volunteer work for the agency. She had no problem asking Sunny for small favors.

One ringing tone, then a cheerful voice announced, "AFTER, Sunny Searle speaking.''

"And after all, Martha Patterson speaking,'' said Martha.

"Martha!'' Sunny exclaimed. "Speak of the devil! I was just going to call you. What's up?''

"How much do you know about the goods and bads of assisted living facilities?''

"Quite a bit. This isn't for you, I hope.''

"Not just yet. It's for a friend.''

"Just checking. What's the story?"

"A single, retired professional woman in her sixties, with lung problems, heart problems, and an intermittent problem with ambulation. I don't know the diagnosis, but sometimes she has to use a wheelchair. She's currently hospitalized with lung and heart problems, and is being told she can't live on her own anymore."

"Rough."

"Just so. She doesn't have anyone to investigate what's available and how well they are managed."

"A good question. I have a file full of reports. Give her my number, and I'll scoop the poop for her, as much as she can stand."

"Many thanks."

"No problem; it's what I do. Now can we talk about something nice?"

"By all means."

"John and I want to take you to dinner."

John.

Martha's mood, already significantly improved by Sunny's good cheer, lightened further. John was John Ainsworth. He had been Martha's supervisor at West Brooklyn. The fact that she was almost twice his age had not affected their professional relationship; John knew his field, and in that field, Martha, for all her forty-plus years of trusts and estates practice, had been as earnest a novice as any brand-new law graduate.

She hadn't seen John in nearly five years, but she knew that he was no longer with West Brooklyn; some years ago his frustration with newly enacted restrictions on Legal Services' practice had sent him off to become a law professor. He and Sunny had been dating at the time she was at West Brooklyn, and it seemed they were still together. Good.

"Dinner sounds good," she said.

"ASAP," Sunny said. "Could you make it tomorrow night?"

Indeed she could.

SHE DOZED OFF on the chaise and woke to find herself struggling groggily with the sense that something was wrong.

Specifically, something had been wrong about that conversation with Irene. For the moment she couldn't put her finger on what it was.

When baffled, drink tea.

She went out to the kitchen, and it was while she was pouring the boiling water onto the tea bag that her mind began to clear. The problem was not with the whole conversation, just the part about depositing the kylix with Arnold for safekeeping when she began to feel ill.

It was the timing. Irene hadn't started to feel seriously ill until Thursday evening. But Arnold had been away on Thursday evening; by the time he had got home on Sunday, Irene had been in the hospital, incommunicado in the ICU, for nearly three days. So when could she have given him the kylix?

Irene's story was seriously implausible. Did she know something about that little pot's wanderings that she didn't want to tell?

THIRTEEN

Trouble

THE TELEPHONE interrupted Martha's contemplation of implausibility. She picked up and announced herself, and heard an uncertainly tenor voice say, "Hello, Ms. Patterson. This is Scott Kaplowitz."

Scott...oh, yes. The older of the Kaplowitzes' boys. She heard a background rumble of traffic; he must have found a working pay phone. Or would the Kaplowitzes have provided him with a cell phone? She thought not; the sound lacked the tin-can quality of those infernal devices. She was grateful to have retired before they became obligatory accessories to professional life.

Scott said, "I hope I'm not bothering you."

"Not at all," she said. "What can I do for you?"

"Well..." His voice cracked from tenor to alto. He cleared his throat and said, "You're a lawyer, right?"

"Retired."

"But if somebody tells you something, you can't tell anyone unless they say it's okay?"

Where did they pick up these half-truths? Perhaps attorney-client confidentiality was an element of those

TV dramas she seldom watched. "It's a little more complicated than that," she said.

"Yeah, well, I guess that's the way with everything. See, what it is, someone I know found out something important, but telling about it could get them in trouble, so they need to talk to someone, like confidentially?"

"I see."

"It's got to be someone that can help them get this information where it should go without getting them in trouble. So I thought, well, you're a lawyer, and you're, you know, sort of involved—"

Involved?

"—so I wondered, could we come to see you? At your place?"

"Who's *we?*" she asked.

"Me and Tyler and Melody."

"Melody Callaghan?"

"Uh-huh. It's, like, tomorrow's her mom's birthday, and her mom let Tyler and me take her shopping. Would it be okay if I brought her up to your place so she could talk to you?"

Oh, dear. "Is she the one who's in trouble?"

"Uh-huh. Tyler doesn't get into that kind of trouble."

"Scott, you know what I'm going to say."

"Yeah, I know. She should talk to her parents. I told her that already. She won't. Her parents are the ones she'd be in trouble with."

Of course; with whom are children more likely to

get into trouble? ''And I suppose she has some reason for not talking to *your* parents?''

''She says my mom would tell her mom.''

''And she thinks I won't?''

''She wants you to be her lawyer so you can't.''

''Scott…''

''I know, but it's serious. She's got to tell *someone* she can trust, and she won't tell her mom and dad, and… I just don't know what to do.''

Martha lowered her voice. ''Does it relate to the shooting of Arnold Stern?''

A hesitation; then, ''Right.''

''And what kind of trouble does she think she'd get into?''

This silence lasted three beats; then he said, ''She broke a rule, and she told a lie, and she says that would get her in the worst trouble she knows.''

''What does she think would happen?''

''She says her dad might send her away to reform school.''

''Scott.''

''I know. It's dumb.''

''Parents can't do that.''

''I know. I told her they can't, but her dad threatened to do it once, when he caught her telling him a lie.''

''Oh, dear.''

''He can say really dumb things when he gets mad.''

''I know. And she believes her daddy.''

''Well, sort of. It's like she doesn't, but she does?''

"I understand. How did you get involved?"

"She told Tyler. He saw it had something to do with Mr. Stern, with him getting killed, and he didn't know what to do, so she said he could tell me if I promised not to tell. Like the big brother thing, you know? And I wanted to talk to somebody sensible, and then I remembered that you're a lawyer and you'd know if there was some way for Melody to tell about—this thing, without it getting back to her mom and dad. And we talked to her, Tyler and I did, and finally she said okay, because it's really bothering her, the way the police keep coming around and questioning her dad."

Without a great deal of hope, Martha gave it one more try:

"She should tell her parents."

"She isn't going to."

"If it's something that might steer the police away from her father, I shouldn't think they'd be too hard on her."

"I told her that. That's why she said I could talk to you."

"I'm to be the go-between."

"That's the idea."

"And you know what she knows, and you think it's important."

"Real important. She's really in a bind. Please. It's too much for me."

An edge of panic in his voice tipped the scale. "All right," she said. "Come on up, and I'll listen."

GUILT NUDGED HER as soon as she hung up. Surely it was inappropriate for Martha Jenkins Patterson, mother and grandmother, to conspire with children against parents. Parents need all the help they could get.

But so do children. Reform school? Good grief. Jeff Callaghan should have his mouth washed out with soap.

FOURTEEN

The Stairwell

MARTHA NO LONGER stocked her kitchen with an eye to children's refreshment. She briefly considered running out for a box of Oreos, but rejected the notion as inappropriate. This gathering wasn't a party; it was by way of being a professional consultation.

The children arrived about twenty minutes later. For her mother's birthday present, Melody had selected a pressed-glass serving bowl. "For salad," she explained.

Martha admired it appropriately, tucked it back into its shopping bag, and set it in the space that the kylix had vacated.

Melody chose to sit on the sofa between Scott and Tyler. Martha took her own seat in the chair she had occupied while Detective White was interviewing her.

"Scott says you want to tell me something," she said.

Melody pulled in her lips and stared at her knees.

Martha waited.

Scott said, "Come on, Mel."

Melody moved her gaze from her knees to Martha's face. "Are you going to tell?"

"Maybe it's something that needs to be told."

"My daddy'll be mad. He'll send me to reform school and they'll whip me."

"He can't do that," said Scott.

"He *said.*"

Scott looked at Martha. *Too much for me,* said his troubled face.

"Scott's right, Melody," said Martha. "That isn't something your father can do."

"He *said.*"

Scott tried again. "He didn't mean it."

Melody's mouth set in a straight line.

Without a pledge of confidentiality, Melody wasn't going to talk. "All right," Martha said reluctantly, "I won't tell unless you say I may."

"Promise?"

The child drove a hard bargain. Martha said, "I promise that I won't tell unless you say I may." If the information was important, she'd try to devise an honorable way out of this vow.

"Cross your heart?"

"Cross my heart." Martha drew an X in the air in front of her chest.

Melody pulled her lips in and stared at her knees.

Martha waited a little longer. Then she said quietly, "I think you want to tell. I think you feel bad about not telling."

"She does feel bad," said Tyler.

Melody jerked her head around and glared at him. "No, I don't," she snapped.

"Do so."

"Ty, put a cork in it," said Scott. "Mel, we came all the way up here so you could tell Ms. Patterson. Now tell her."

Melody looked at him. Then she looked at Martha. Then, as if a dam had breached, words came tumbling out like pebbles in a flood-stage mountain stream: "I went in the stairs, and I saw a man."

Ah, there was the problem: the stairs. The house rules placed the stairwell, the corridors, and the elevator off-limits to unaccompanied children. The Callaghans were apparently to be counted among those parents who were hard-put to enforce that rule.

"Were you by yourself?" Martha asked.

Melody nodded.

"She does it a lot," Tyler volunteered.

"Do not."

"Do so." Tyler looked across at Martha. "She does it when she's coming up to our place. If her mom is in back somewhere, she opens their door and rings the bell, and then she tells her mom that my mom's waiting to take her up, and then she comes up the stairs, and when she gets up to our place she tells my mom her mom brought her up and went back down already."

When Martha had sorted out the moms, she asked Tyler, "Doesn't your mother notice that Melody's mother isn't there?"

Scott said, "When Ty knows she's coming up, he

makes up some story to keep our mom in the back and he goes to the door himself.''

''Then he teases me about being bad,'' said Melody.

One must not, must absolutely *not,* express one's sneaking admiration for the ingenuity displayed by this pair of cooped-up eight-year-olds in devising and pulling off such an elaborate piece of deception. ''Well,'' Martha said, ''it is bad. It could be dangerous.''

''I'm *careful!''* Melody protested. ''I listen before I open the door, and then I sneak in and look, and if there's anybody there I go home and let Mommy take me up. Like I did when I saw the man.''

The man, yes. The man was the point of this consultation. ''Where were you when you saw him?''

''In the *stairs.* I *said.''*

''I'm sorry. I mean what floor were you on?''

''Oh. Mine. Sixteen.''

One floor below this one. Therefore one floor below Arnold Stern's apartment.

Martha tried to recall how well-developed an eight-year-old's sense of time was. ''Do you remember what day that was?''

''The day Tyler's mom took us to the park.''

''We saw you out on the plaza,'' Tyler offered. ''You said you'd help me get a dog.''

That had been last Sunday. Last Sunday was the day Arnold Stern had been killed.

Melody's clandestine visit to the stairwell might be important. If important, it could have been dangerous. A twinge of anxiety tightened Martha's chest: it might still be dangerous. "Do you know who the man was?" she asked.

After a little hesitation, Melody shook her head.

"Did he see you?"

"How do I know? I don't have somebody else's eyes."

Tyler snickered.

Melody scowled. "Well, I don't."

"Did you see his face?" Martha asked.

"Oh." Melody's frown disappeared. "No. He was going downstairs. I just saw his head." She swept her hand from the top of her head to the nape of her neck.

The telephone beside the chaise warbled. Martha's muscles tightened with the conditioned impulse to answer it, but she smothered the urge and said over the second ring, "You didn't see his face, just the back of his head?"

"I *said*."

"I'm just making sure I understand. Can you tell me if you saw him before that? In the hall, I mean, going into the stairs?"

Melody's *"No!"* nearly drowned out the third ring. "I'm *careful!* If I saw him go in, I wouldn't go in!"

Fourth ring, then Martha's recorded voice reciting the *Please-leave-your-name-and-number* message, then the click of a hang-up.

"Do you remember what color his hair was?" Martha asked.

"Black." Melody looked at Scott. "Not as black as yours, and it was wavy."

As her story had emerged, Scott had relaxed. Now

he grinned at Melody and said, "American hair." His was jet black and stick-straight; the Kaplowitzes had traveled to China to adopt him.

"I was going up to Tyler's to go to the park," Melody said, "and I saw the man in the stairs and I went home and Mommy took me up in the elevator. And I told Tyler and he kept saying I'm bad."

"You are bad," Tyler said.

"Am not."

Tyler obviously needed attention. Martha looked across at him and asked, "Do you remember that day?"

"Yep," he said. "Her dad was downstairs yelling...."

"He *wasn't* yelling!"

"Yes, he was. And my mom said, 'That doesn't sound too nice. Let's see if Melody wants to go to the park,' and she called and her mom brought her up, and I said 'Why didn't you come up the stairs,' and she said she was going to but a man was in the stairs so she didn't."

A trial lawyer couldn't ask for a more complete and succinct corroboration.

"Don't tell," said Melody.

"Did I promise?" said Martha.

"Yes."

"I keep promises."

ON THE WAY OUT the door, the shopping bag's handles clutched in her fist, Melody turned back. "He *wasn't* yelling," she said. "He was having a dis*cuss*ion."

FIFTEEN

Cloak and Dagger

MARTHA SAW the children into the elevator and returned to her own apartment in a quandary. Someone should tell the police about the man in the stairwell, but Martha, the only adult in the know, had promised not to tell.

The telephone warbled once more as she was pondering the problem. She suppressed annoyance, arranged herself on the chaise, and picked up. A mature female voice identified itself as belonging to Helen Taubensee.

For a moment, still preoccupied with secrets that must be disclosed, Martha couldn't remember who Helen Taubensee was. The name was not unfamiliar—oh, yes. Helen Taubensee was a member of the co-op board. She was, in fact one of the three members who were up for reelection.

"Yes, Ms. Taubensee," Martha said.

"I hope I'm not interrupting anything."

Since the only thing being interrupted was an inaccurate notion that she needed to resume her nap, Martha said, "Not at all."

"I apologize for hanging up on your answering machine. I didn't want to say anything that could be overheard."

"I'm the only one here," said Martha.

"Then I'll get to the point. I understand you have an interest in serving on the board."

That again. "The subject has been discussed."

"And you haven't ruled out the possibility?"

"No."

"Good. I hear good things about you. There's some co-op business I'd like you to know about. It's rather tricky, and for reasons of security I don't want to spread it around the board, but I don't want to tackle it alone."

More secrets? Curiosity began to fray the edge of Martha's weariness. "I'm listening," she said.

"This may come across as paranoia, but I think it would be better not to talk about it on the phone. Or anywhere in or near the building, for that matter. Do you know the Brooklyn Promenade? In Brooklyn Heights?"

"Yes, I do," Martha said. West Brooklyn Legal Services, where she had worked briefly some years ago, was a few blocks from the public space (called the Esplanade by a handful of purists, the Promenade by the rest of the known universe) that had been constructed over a stretch of the Brooklyn-Queens Expressway overlooking Manhattan's financial district across the harbor. It had occasionally been a destination of her lunch-hour walks.

Helen Taubensee said, "I'm meeting someone there

at noon tomorrow. I'd like you to take part in the conversation. Could you possibly meet us there? Twelve noon, at the north end. The Watchtower end.''

Martha hesitated. This invitation sounded rather like one of those devices dear to the writers of Gothic thrillers, a mysterious summons luring the idiot heroine into darkness and mortal peril.

The notion was absurd. Noon was not midnight, and the Esplanade was not a deserted castle. Every noon, dozens—perhaps hundreds—of working people gathered on its benches to enjoy the view while they ate their take-out lunches. Her weariness didn't altogether vanish, but it contracted to a hard little knob just behind her eyes, and curiosity ballooned to fill the space it had vacated.

"Yes," she said. "Yes, all right.''

MOMENTS LATER, while fatigue and hunger were debating the relative merits of trying to resume her nap versus going out for something to eat, the phone rang again. She sighed and picked up.

"It's me again," said Irene Xendopoulis. Her wheeze had not abated.

"I owe you a call," said Martha. "I said I'd try to find out more about assisted living facilities, and I have failed to report back. I apologize. Hold on, I have a number for you to call—someone who specializes in such matters.''

"Many thanks. Now I've dreamed up something else to pester you with. Please say no if it's too much.''

"Tell me what it is."

"One way or another, I'm going to have to give up the apartment. I'll be getting rid of a lot of my furniture, and I need someone to collect the personal papers out of my desk. Peter—my nephew, you met him—is helping with the furniture, but this isn't really his thing. If you'll do it, I'll pay your hourly fee."

"Oh, nonsense, we're neighbors," said Martha. "How shall I get into your apartment?"

"Would it be too much to ask you to come and collect my keys?"

"Not at all. Tomorrow afternoon?"

"That'd be good. Visiting hours start at two."

BELATEDLY WONDERING if she would recognize Helen Taubensee outside the context of a shareholders' meeting, Martha rode the subway to downtown Brooklyn. She climbed the stairs to the street and walked past the small shops and posh row houses of Montague Street, and then past the lunch-hour loungers and lunchers on the Esplanade.

Her worry was needless; as soon as she saw the two figures in the distance, silhouetted against the massive stone pier of the Brooklyn Bridge, she recognized one of them as the hefty, well-tailored woman she had last seen sitting among the board members at shareholders' meetings. The man with her was fortyish, medium-sized, and muscular, dressed in jeans and a navy polo shirt. When she got closer, she saw MACKIE stitched on the pocket of his shirt.

"Thank you for coming," said the woman as Martha approached. "Ms. Patterson, this is Michael McGarrity."

Martha extended her hand. "Mr. McGarrity."

"Mackie," he said. His handshake was firm.

"And I'm Martha."

"Helen," said Helen Taubensee. "Shall we sit down?"

"I can't take a long time with this," said Mackie. "My foreman keeps an eye on the clock."

"We won't keep you long," Helen said. "Just tell Martha what you told me."

He glanced over his shoulder. Martha found herself looking back along the Esplanade, as well. No one was within earshot.

"Sorry," he said, "This thing has me a little spooked." He puffed out a breath. "Martha, Helen says you live in her building. Over on Eighth Street, just had a lobby renovation?"

"Yes."

"Connors and Whitaker handled the job?"

"I believe that was the firm."

"You ever ask yourself why it was Connors and Whitaker got the job?"

"No, I can't say that I did." Martha glanced at Helen. "I assumed that they submitted the most attractive bid."

Helen nodded.

Mackie looked over his shoulder again, then dropped his voice to a murmur. "Ever ask yourself how they knew to submit the best bid?"

"No," said Martha. "Are you suggesting that they had inside information?"

"You might say." Another glance over his shoulder. Nearly whispering now, he said, "Ever hear of kickbacks?"

Martha looked at Helen. "Why am I hearing this?" she asked.

"Just listen," said Helen.

Martha looked back at Mackie. "Who got the kickback?"

"You'll keep my name out of this?"

Heartily tired of secrets, Martha said, "Not if you want something to come of this meeting. You seem to be on the verge of accusing someone of a criminal act. If it were to go to trial, you would very likely be subpoenaed to testify."

He shifted his weight from one foot to the other.

"What's your line of work?" she asked.

"Carpenter."

"Are you afraid you'll be fired if your employer identifies you as the whistle-blower?"

"I'm not working for them anymore." He dropped his voice so low that Martha had to lean in to hear him. "I'm not worried about getting fired—I'm worried about getting shot." Yet another glance over his shoulder. If the man wasn't frightened, he was a competent actor.

"Shot by whom?" Martha asked.

"There's somebody on your board of directors named—Young?" He nearly whispered the name.

"Yolanda Young?"

He patted the air in a *keep-it-down* gesture. "Been in her apartment lately?" he asked.

"I have, as a matter of fact."

"Check out the carpet and the countertop?"

"Well, I think the countertop is granite. I don't normally pay much attention to carpets unless they're garish. It did look new."

"Next time, take a better look, and then take a look at what we put in the lobby."

His indirection was beginning to annoy her. She spelled it out—albeit quietly: "Are you saying she told your former employer what the other bids were, so that they could underbid by a few dollars? And they paid her off by installing some items in her apartment?"

Mackie moved his shoulders impatiently. "Top of the line items. The project manager over-ordered, and after the lobby was done, he sent a crew to install the surplus in her place."

"Free of charge?"

"You got it. She did tip pretty good."

But apparently not enough to keep Mackie Mc-Garrity quiet. "That was many months ago," Martha said. "Why are you telling us now?"

"Want to do the right thing."

"That's public-spirited of you. Is there any other reason?"

He shrugged. "Not really."

"Why aren't you working for that firm anymore? Did you get fired?"

"No way. I bailed. The manager put the kibosh on

a promotion I was due, so I bailed. The new job's better.''

''Why are you afraid you'll be shot?''

Again that *keep-it-down* gesture. ''See, here's the story. I got this new job, and I wanted to do the right thing. So I called the president of your board and told him about what's-her-face getting the carpet and granite. He said thanks, he'd look into it. Next thing I know, it's on the news, somebody shot him.''

''I see.''

''Yeah. Maybe I'm putting two and two together and getting five, but let me tell you, I don't like it when somebody's walking behind me at night.''

''Do you have any proof of all this?''

''Just take a good look around the lobby and then scope out that apartment. Oh, and I forgot. Check out that screen at the corner of her kitchen counter.''

''I mean documentary proof.''

He shrugged. ''Try comparing the designer's specs and the delivery records.'' He looked at a watch on his wrist. ''Listen, I gotta go.''

''WHAT DO YOU THINK?'' Helen Taubensee asked after Mackie McGarrity had trotted off.

''Why me?'' asked Martha.

''It seemed like a good idea to bring in someone who's interested but not involved.''

It didn't seem like a particularly good idea to Martha. But for good or bad, here she was. ''I did notice a little bronze screen like the one in front of the elevators,'' she said, ''but it's so small, I suspect it was a piece of scrap. Where in the lobby did they install polished granite countertop?''

"The mantel over the fireplace.''

Martha felt her mind skitter away from the thought of the lobby fireplace. She had once taken part in a distressing conversation in front of its fake logs and gas flame—a conversation so disturbing that ever after she had steered clear of that side of the lobby.

"What does Mackie expect to get out of telling this story?'' she asked.

"You don't believe him?''

"My mind is open. I'd just like to know what's in it for him. Is it revenge for failing to get the promotion?''

"Haven't you ever wanted to sandbag a supervisor?''

"But why tell us? If he thinks there was fraud, he should tell his story to the police.''

"He's afraid.''

"That he'll get shot? That seems far-fetched.''

"Arnold got shot,'' said Helen. "Think about the sequence. Mackie told Arnold Yolanda got a kickback; Arnold said he'd look into it; Arnold was shot.''

"I'm sorry,'' said Martha, "I don't find that very convincing. Even if Arnold took the matter to the DA, and the DA decided there was enough evidence to prosecute the firm that did the work, the penalty would very likely be no more serious than a fine. I believe many firms budget fines as a regular cost of doing business.''

"Mackie isn't thinking along those lines," said Helen. "What about Yolanda Young herself?"

Martha had been avoiding thinking about Yolanda Young. "If anyone took the matter to the DA," she conceded, "I suppose there might be repercussions."

"Like losing her job," said Helen. "Arnold would have taken it to the DA. He was a straight arrow. He had that disgusting way of smarming around women, but he was no crook. He would have been outraged to know a colleague on the board was doing something underhanded."

"Are you sure? The building must have benefited from the low bid."

"Not so. There were big cost overruns. In the end, we'd have been better off with a more realistic bidder. He was upset with the way it worked out. I can imagine him confronting Yolanda when Mackie told him that story. She has a temper. What if they had a fight and he got out the gun to protect himself—it was his own gun, wasn't it?"

"So I'm told."

"What if she got it away from him?..." Helen broke off. "Tell me this is crazy."

"No crazier than anything else that's going on," said Martha. "But if it will relieve your mind, I find some problems with your scenario."

"Tell me. Please."

"To begin with, on the day Arnold was shot, someone telephoned Yolanda and threatened her with death if she didn't stop messing with people's lives."

"How do you know?"

"I was there."

"Where?"

"In her apartment."

"I didn't know you knew her that well."

"I don't. She heard I might be running for the board, and she invited me down to tell me that the air-conditioner breakdown wasn't the board's fault and I should leave it out of my campaign."

"She's got a nerve."

"May I quote you?"

"No."

"While I was there, she got a call that seemed to disturb her. When she hung up, I asked what was wrong, and she said the caller told her she should stop messing up people's lives or she'd die."

"That's dramatic. Did you hear it? The actual words?"

"No. Just her end, and what she told me afterwards."

"Could she have made it up? What if she'd just shot Arnold and thought she'd divert suspicion by pretending she was being threatened, too?"

"I don't think so. The phone did ring."

"Maybe it was a telemarketer, and she pretended it was a threat."

"Helen, do you write novels?"

"Advertising pays better."

"Isn't that fiction?"

"I'll pretend I didn't hear that."

"I think it happened the way she said. She was disturbed, and I don't think she was pretending. Oh, I forgot another detail. As soon as she hung up, she dialed again, and after a little wait she said, 'Arnold, call me!' Apparently she didn't know he was dead.''

''She could have been faking that.''

''I just don't think so.''

''She's devious. 'Messing up our lives' is the way those two gay girls were talking when we turned down their nursery. What if she invented the threat and used those words in order to implicate them? Did she say if it was a man or a woman?''

''She said she couldn't tell. She thought it was someone disguising his voice. His or her. Helen, I don't think she invented anything. She was very much disturbed.''

''Anyone can act disturbed.''

''But I don't think one can turn pale at will.''

''Well... Oh, never mind. You think the police should hear this story.''

''Yes, of course. And I don't think Mackie is going to tell them, so it's up to you.''

Helen frowned. ''Before I start shooting off my mouth, I'd better take a look at those order forms and bills.''

SIXTEEN

Irene II

HELEN TAUBENSEE LEFT the Esplanade by the nearest route. Martha remembered a Greek restaurant she had discovered while working at West Brooklyn Legal Services, so she walked back to where she had entered the Esplanade and trudged up Montague Street past the houses to the shops.

The place was still in business. She refueled with a pita pocket stuffed with hummus and falafel, but remembering that she was scheduled to have dinner with Sunny and John, drew the line at dessert.

Walking back to Lower Manhattan across the Brooklyn Bridge, she decided that the precaution had been unnecessary; the walk against a stiff breeze was using up at least as many calories as a serving of baklava would have provided. When the bridge came to earth across the street from City Hall Park, she gave up and flagged a cab.

The short ride provided enough leisure for another problem with Helen's theory to cross her mind. If Arnold and Yolanda had been as close as everyone seemed to assume—and as Yolanda's attempt to call

Arnold after the anonymous death threat seemed to indicate—then Arnold would surely already have known about, and found nothing wrong with, her acquisition of the new carpet and countertop. Therefore Mackie McGarrity's call to Arnold would have posed no threat to Yolanda.

IRENE WAS SITTING upright against a mound of pillows. Her need for continued care was obvious; her color was doughy, and each breath was effortful. A mask attached by a hose to an oxygen tank dangled within easy reach.

But Irene mustered a weak smile, and, picking a key ring off the nightstand, wheezed, "Hi, good neighbor. This is a load off my mind."

"It's little enough," said Martha.

"Your little is my lot. The boy's a trouper, but his field is furniture. You're the paper person. I wish you'd let me pay you for your time. I'm paying Peter."

"Well, that's between you and him. I will not accept payment for a neighborly favor."

"Then I'll shut up about it. It shouldn't take you too long. God knows, the boy can use a little spare income. He got suckered into that day-trading scam a few years back—remember that?—and I don't think he's got out of the hole yet. But I'm babbling about somebody else's business. Forget I said anything."

"Said what?" Martha took the keys. "Will he need these?"

"No, I had him make his own." A spasm of chesty

coughing shook Irène. When she recovered her breath, she said, "Do you know what that boy did? He took himself over to my apartment and packed a bag with the nicest things he could find." More coughing. "You can't wear your own things in the ICU, but it's the thought that counts, isn't it? I mean, we all have impulses, but we don't all act on them." She tried to chuckle; the attempt ended in more coughing.

And it's just as well we don't all act on impulse, thought Martha, *or more of us might have been suckered into Internet day trading.* "I'm afraid I'm tiring you," she said.

"I'm tiring me. Sit down. Company won't kill me, boredom will. Are they still trying to find out who shot Arnold?"

She sounded more curious than agitated. All the same, Martha spoke with caution. "I haven't heard anything new," she said.

"Are they *cherchez*-ing any *femmes?*"

Her mind full of Yolanda Young, Martha asked, "Do you have any *femmes* to suggest?"

"Aren't there are always *femmes?*"

"Well, Lila did say he flirted."

"Oh, her. He liked people who shared his interests. She wasn't one of them."

"And you were."

"He should have been an archaeologist."

Martha decided to treat the remark as an opening. "Speaking of archaeology," she said, "the other day you said something I didn't understand."

"Only one thing?"

"It was about that Greek pot of yours."

"Oh, my little orphaned kylix. I hope that detective is looking after it. I hid it from myself and didn't look at it from one year to the next—don't ask why or I'll bore myself by answering—but it's worth a lot of money. If New York's finest ever give it back to me, I ought to sell it."

The speech left her panting, and it was not without a twinge of guilt that Martha persisted. "What confused me," she said, "was that you said you had given the kylix to Arnold for safekeeping when you became ill, but I can't figure out when you had a chance to give it to him."

Irene drew a breath. It triggered more coughing, this spasm drier and longer. She reached for the oxygen mask and cupped it over her nose and mouth.

The question wasn't going to be answered. Martha said, "I should let you rest."

Irene held the mask an inch away from her face and spoke faintly. "I'm sorry."

"It's my fault for tiring you." Martha got to her feet. "How will I know which are the right documents?"

Irene laid the mask aside. "All the papers in the desk. Peter can have the hardware. You know, pencils, paper clips, that kind of thing. No, save out one stapler. The little black one. It's my favorite."

FEELING FAR WEARIER than the day's exercise warranted, Martha flagged another cab in front of the hospital.

Irene was lying.

That last fit of coughing, which had ended the conversation just when Irene was going to have to explain when (if ever) she had given the kylix to Arnold for safekeeping, had sounded different from the earlier spasms. Drier and less phlegmy.

Faked.

Martha had thought it before; now she was sure: Irene knew more about that wandering pot than she was willing to say.

SHE WAS STILL preoccupied with that conviction when she entered her building, and as she crossed the lobby, a little memory flickered across her mind. It was of something that had happened while they were waiting for the ambulance to take Irene to the hospital. In the context of medical emergency, it was a small thing, and that smallness was probably the reason she hadn't remembered it until just now, when her visit to Irene was followed so closely by her entry into the lobby.

Irene had handed her keys to Peter and sent him up to her apartment to get something she had forgotten. And this was what Martha was just now remembering: as Peter was sprinting across the lobby to the elevator, Irene had called after him, "Peter, it's all right." She hadn't defined the *it* that was *all right*. Peter was evidently supposed to know what *it* was.

Martha was already convinced that Irene had not given the kylix to Arnold. Now she wondered if Peter—whom Irene herself declared to be in financial straits—might have taken it, and if Irene knew he had taken it, and if, down here in the lobby that night, afraid that she was facing death and cherishing her nephew as her only remaining relative, she had called out to tell him that it was *all right* for him to have it?

The elevator arrived. Martha stepped in and pressed 17. As she began her ascent, her powerful sense of logic protested that four words gasped out by a sick woman in crisis did not provide an adequate basis for supposing that Peter Sanders, however impoverished, had stolen a valuable artifact from his doting aunt. That fantasy did nothing to explain how the thing had got into Arnold's apartment.

Nor did the supposed wanderings of the kylix appear to have anything to do with Mackie McGarrity's kickback story. That story, Martha felt, was a good deal more probable than her own vaporings about Irene's devoted nephew and that wretched pot.

She still had trouble, however, understanding how the kickback story meshed with Yolanda Young's anonymous phone call...unless Helen Taubensee's suggestion was on the money, and Yolanda had invented that melodramatic death threat to deflect suspicion from herself.

Could one turn pale at will?

Thoroughly confused, Martha stepped out of the elevator into the seventeenth-floor corridor. She would have given a great deal just then for the power to cancel the recent past and encounter Arnold Stern just coming out his door.

She had locked her own door behind her and was

putting the kettle on for tea when she remembered something that all these confused speculations had driven far to the back of her mind:

Yolanda Young had disappeared.

SEVENTEEN

Interlude

JOHN AND SUNNY WERE waiting in the bar when Martha arrived at the chattery, checked-tablecloth restaurant on the Upper West Side that they had chosen for this interlude. Martha badly needed an interlude.

John greeted her with a not unwelcome New York-style peck on the cheek. Since she had last seen him, his fair hair had receded an inch or two on either side above his forehead, but because much of his attractiveness depended on agility of mind and body, the onset of male-pattern baldness did nothing to impair it. A good many years ago, he had abandoned an unprofitable theatrical career to become a lawyer; the aura remained.

They were shown to their table; they ordered; Sunny looked at John; John looked at Sunny.

"You tell her," said Sunny.

John looked at Martha. "We're getting married," he said.

"I wondered if that might be it," she said.

"And you're thinking it's about time."

She was thinking exactly that. Once, years before,

Sunny had expressed reservations about exposing her thirteen-year-old daughter to John's powerful appeal on a daily basis. Martha had thought the qualms unjustified, but she had respected the anxieties of a single mother. The qualms must have departed along with the daughter, who was now a freshman in one of the SUNY colleges upstate.

So, yes; it was high time. But all she said was, "Did I say anything?"

"You'll come, I hope."

"Of course. Just tell me when and where."

"Don't laugh," John said.

"September," said Sunny, "pretty soon after Labor Day. The exact date depends on some other stuff. You'll get it in writing. In Central Park, west side near the Seventy-second Street entrance. We'll show you the site after dinner."

"Wild horses wouldn't stop me." No, this situation demanded an uncliched response. "Stampeding zebras wouldn't stop me," she amended.

John said, "The zoo's on the other side of the park, so you're unlikely to be put to the test."

"I'll clear the entire month of September," said Martha. "Do you need a permit to get married in the park?"

"To speak a few quiet words among an orderly gathering of friends?" said John. "I shouldn't think so. A marriage license, yes. An officiant, yes. A park-use permit, probably no."

"We're checking," said Sunny. "I've heard that if

we keep the attendance under twenty, we won't need one.''

''It's a good deal less damaging than playing Frisbee,'' said John. ''Which we may also do. And that is quite enough about us. For the moment. What's doing with you?''

She hesitated before answering. A murder was what was doing with her, but she had had quite enough of that. She hastily ran up a mental wall between thought and speech and said, ''Freelance research and the customary New York entertainments.'' Better prosaic than obsessively sensational.

But before she could launch into a harmless account of her trip to Phillips Landing, John's expression told her he had picked up her discomfort. ''Do you miss clients and courts?'' he asked.

She ignored the subtext and concentrated on the actual words. Did she miss clients and courts? She had missed them at first, but now, having inadvertently taken on an eight-year-old quasi-client, she would be glad to be spared the burden. She pushed that thought behind the wall and said, ''Not intolerably. Do you?''

''Not intolerably. Law students are unexpectedly amusing. And you may or may not be surprised to learn that I've stuck a toe back into the theater.''

''I'm sure one misses it.''

''Like missing crack, I'm told. Anyway. Three years or so ago a local amateur group was looking for a director. Church basement, three productions a year, audience consisting of mommas and poppas, uncles and aunts, girlfriends and boyfriends, loyal spouses.

Payment in doughnuts, coffee, and the theatrical fix. It couldn't have been better timed. I was slogging through a slough of despond. Congress was hostile to the good, true, and beautiful, and interpersonal friction at the office was rubbing me raw. I expect you know what I'm talking about.''

"I do."

"Or you'd probably still be there. Yes, well. I answered the ad, and they took me on."

"Congratulations."

"Thank you."

"And did it drain the despond from the slough?"

"It helped."

"It helped everybody," Sunny said. "By his third production they were playing to standing room and getting reviewed."

"In a local giveaway weekly," said John.

"You should have sent me a flyer," said Martha.

"Didn't you get one? I gave your name to the kid who does our PR."

"Who ostensibly does their PR," said Sunny.

"I'll mail the next one personally," said John.

"I'd like that. And by the way, I've been saving a theatrical question for you."

"You have but to ask."

"If a script calls for emotional disturbance, is there a way for an actor to will himself to turn pale?"

"Good question. Stanislavsky would tell him to imagine the most terrifying situation he'd ever been in, and hope the bloodstream would follow suit."

"Does it work?"

"It might. I've never had occasion to try."

"I don't suppose a layman would know how."

"If he pulled it off, he should start taking auditions."

"I see. Thank you for sharing your expertise. I'm curious; is directing an adequate substitute for acting?"

"It does pretty well. Actually, the other month I was allowed to face the footlights. We were doing *Candide* and our Marchbanks developed laryngitis on opening night. We don't have the talent resources for understudies." Again he ran his hand across his thinning hair. "I'm a little long in the tooth to play a callow young poet, but I had to step into the part."

"It's too bad you weren't there," said Sunny. "You'd have sworn he was nineteen."

"Easy for her to say," said John. "Do you have any idea how hot a wig can get under stage lights?"

EIGHTEEN

Mother

THE EVENING HAD BEEN agreeable. The night was another story. In spite of going to bed a couple of hours past her usual bedtime, Martha could not fall asleep. As soon as she began to drift off, ruminations about the grisly death in the next-door apartment came crawling out from behind the wall where she had shoved them, dragging with them the kylix and the still unanswered question: How had that wretched pot got into the Sterns' apartment?

She turned from her left side to her right; she squeezed her eyelids shut.

Her pillow developed a lump under her cheek. She raised herself on one elbow, punched the pillow flat, and laid her head back down. After a while she turned from her right side to her left.

The question had embedded itself in her thinking as firmly as a tick clung to a dog's skin. It had been a long time since a troublesome thought had clung so obstinately.

She turned from her left side to her right. She couldn't find comfortable positions for her arms.

She gave up on physical comfort and tried diverting her mind to an alternative question. Why, she asked herself, was she persisting in this profitless rumination? Irene herself had offered quite a plausible explanation: Irene insisted that she had asked Arnold to look after the kylix for her. Why not accept Irene's story? It was, after all, Irene's pot.

Just where her hip rested on the mattress, Martha's nightgown had twisted into a lump. She struggled out of bed, shook the nightgown straight, laid back down, and closed her eyes again.

Yes, Irene's story was plausible on its face, but it was not plausible enough to overcome the grounds for disbelief that Martha had already tabulated. She couldn't shake the conviction that Peter had taken the kylix. Or, at least, that Irene believed he had, and that she had made up the giving-it-to-Arnold story to protect him.

So—assume that Peter had taken the kylix. The question, slightly modified, remained: How had the kylix got from Peter's hands to the shelf that held Lila's ceramic collection?

And this time her mind managed to produce an answer. It was, to be sure, only a tentative answer and would probably not stand up to close scrutiny, but it was disconcerting enough to distract her from the search for a comfortable position.

What if Irene had told her good friend Arnold that the kylix had disappeared, and in her agitation, had blurted out her suspicion of Peter? What if, upon returning from upstate on that fatal Sunday afternoon, and discovering that Irene was in the hospital, Arnold had confronted Peter, retrieved the kylix from him, and placed it with Lila's ceramics until he could return it to Irene? What if the confrontation had become so acrimonious that Arnold had produced that wretched gun, thinking to protect himself? What if Peter, young, healthy, and with a reputation to protect, had wrested the gun away and, whether accidentally or deliberately, pulled the trigger?

Peter had been in the building on that fatal Sunday; he had come out the door, in a tearing hurry, while Martha was chatting with Ruth Kaplowitz in the plaza.

And Peter had dark wavy hair.

It didn't take long for Martha's analytical mind to notice a problem with the timing. This hypothesis required Irene to have told Arnold that the kylix was missing at some time before she was taken to the hospital on Thursday night. But Arnold hadn't been shot until three days later, on Sunday afternoon; therefore, Arnold's hypothetical confrontation with Peter must have taken place on Sunday afternoon. But Peter surely wouldn't have been carrying the wretched pot with him on Sunday, so how would Arnold have been able to take it from him?

And it was not only the timing; the geography didn't work either. The shooting had taken place in Arnold's apartment. Why on earth would Peter have gone to Arnold's apartment on that Sunday afternoon?

Martha's mind was quite capable of inventing further hypotheses to explain those anomalies, and for a few minutes it set about doing so. The explanations it produced, however, were improbable to the point of absurdity, and very soon she ordered it to abandon the task.

Still, articulating the theory and then shooting it full of holes (a figure of speech that Martha wished hadn't occurred to her) had apparently satisfied that obstinately questioning mind, for at last she dropped into sleep.

THE TELEPHONE woke her. Strips of daylight shone bright between the slats of the Venetian blinds, and the temperature in the bedroom was closer to hot than to warm. She raised herself from her sweaty pillow on one elbow and saw the red numbers on the clock on the bedside table flip from 8:03 to 8:04. For Martha, a lifelong morning person, this was late.

She picked up the phone before the third ring.

It was Vanessa Callaghan. "I have to talk to you," she said. "Can I come up?"

This had to be about Melody and the stairwell. The refreshing interlude with young friends was over.

"Now?" Martha asked.

"Well..." Vanessa's voice lost force. "If it isn't..."

Parental anxiety recognizes no timetable. "No, it's all right," Martha said. "Give me half an hour."

THE DEPTH OF the easy chair made perching difficult, but Vanessa managed to perch. Her hands were clenched on top of her knees, which were bare beneath shorts. She declined Martha's offer of tea.

"The kids came to see you yesterday," she said.

"Yes, they did," said Martha.

"What for?"

"They wanted to discuss something with me."

"Discuss what?"

Martha had expected this conversation to be difficult. It seemed likely to live up to her expectation. "I'm sorry, I can't tell you," she said. "I promised to keep it confidential."

"Confidential!"

"Yes."

"Melody's *eight years old!*"

"Yes."

"I'm her *mother.*"

"Yes, and that does create a conflict for me. However, I made a promise, and that takes precedence."

"But...she's just a little girl."

Martha did her best to speak gently. "I do not take promises lightly."

Vanessa stretched her fingers wide apart, knotted them together again, and said, "I don't understand what you think you're doing."

"It's quite simple," Martha said. "Your daughter wanted to talk to me in confidence, and I promised her that I'd keep her confidence."

"But..." Vanessa broke off. Then, her voice several tones less shrill, she asked, "Is it about my birthday present? I know Scotty was taking her shopping. If that's all it is..."

Martha shook her head.

"Oh, *don't!*" Vanessa's voice rose again. "Don't

play lawyer games with me. I have a little girl who's up half the night with nightmares. My little girl. What's she afraid of?''

Reform school. Martha didn't say it; instead, she said, ''Why don't you ask her?

''I did. She won't tell me.'' A moment passed. ''Is it about Arnold?''

The accuracy of the guess should probably not have surprised Martha, but for a moment it did. She took another moment to think about her response. Her promise to Melody, she decided, did not preclude a qualified answer. ''It may be,'' she said.

''Oh, rats. She knew, didn't she?''

''Knew what?''

''Oh.'' Vanessa sagged. The movement was not relaxation, it was retreat. ''Nothing.''

''Knew what?'' Martha repeated.

''Nothing,'' Vanessa said. ''Really, nothing. I just...I'm just trying to figure out what's got her so upset.''

What Vanessa thought Melody knew wasn't going to emerge. Not in this conversation. ''If this discussion is to have any chance of continuing,'' Martha said, ''Melody will have to be part of it. Where is she?''

''Up at Ruth's.'' A bit defensively, Vanessa added, ''They get up early.''

''One does, with children,'' Martha said peaceably. ''Why don't you get her?''

VANESSA DIDN'T PERCH this time; she sat back in the chair to make a lap. Melody's bare legs dangled across her bare thighs.

"Daddy'll send me to reform school," she said. Her voice was muffled in Vanessa's shoulder.

"No, he won't," said Vanessa.

"He said."

"He didn't mean it."

"And they'll whip me."

"Nobody's going to whip you."

Melody squirmed her face free. "He *said!*"

"He didn't mean it, sweetie. You know Daddy sometimes says things he doesn't mean. Like a joke."

"He wasn't laughing."

"I didn't say it *was* a joke, I said it was *like* a joke. Not a very funny one. Nobody's going to send you anywhere, and nobody's going to whip you."

"Daddy said." This time Melody's tone was uncertain.

"He didn't mean it. Daddy just says things like that when you don't tell the truth."

"Then *he* isn't telling the truth."

"It's just because he loves you and doesn't want you to get hurt. Nobody's going to send you anywhere."

"Promise?"

"I promise."

"Cross your heart?"

"Cross my heart and hope to die."

Melody buried her face again. Almost inaudibly, she said, "I went in the stairs."

Martha hadn't realized she'd been holding her breath until she found herself letting it out.

"Well." Vanessa rubbed her cheek against the top

of Melody's head. "I sort of figured it was something like that."

"And I saw a man."

Martha saw Vanessa tense. "What happened?"

Still muffled, Melody said, "Don't tell Daddy."

"All Daddy wants is for you to tell the truth."

Melody squirmed her face free. "Don't *tell* him."

Vanessa said, "All right."

"Cross your heart?"

"Cross my heart and hope to die."

The dam, having been breached once before, gave way again, and once more the story came spilling out: the sixteenth-floor landing, the man descending the stairs, the dark wavy hair.

"Was he somebody you know?" Vanessa asked.

Melody shook her head.

"Did he see you?"

"I don't know. I didn't see his face. I went out and came right home."

"You were a good girl to come right home."

"Tyler says I'm bad."

"Tyler's a big tease. You were a good girl to come right home, and you're a good girl to tell me about it." Vanessa shifted forward in the chair. "Okay, sweetie, time to go home."

"No."

"Yes. It's time. Ms. Patterson has things to do."

"*No!* I don't want to go *home!* I want to go back to *Tyler's*. We were watching cartoons and you inter-*rupt*ed us!"

NINETEEN

Paul Tells A Tale

VANESSA HAD PAINTED herself into the same corner from which Melody's confession had extricated Martha: to make any contribution toward clearing Jeff, the story about the man in the stairwell must be told to the police, but in order to hear the story at all, she had had to promise not to tell it to anyone.

Martha turned the locks behind mother and daughter and rejoiced that the problem was no longer hers alone.

The conversation had exhausted her. These days, everything was exhausting her. She considered tea, rejected the idea, went back into the bedroom, and, although she had no hope of further sleep, laid down fully dressed on top of the unmade bed. In her teens and twenties, sleeping late on Saturdays had been easy, but parenthood had destroyed that facility. Horizontal rest, however, even without sleep, should help....

She jerked awake.

The bedside clock said it was 10:19 a.m. Something

had awakened her, and her head was thick with unfinished sleep.

A voice. She had heard a voice. She had heard it only faintly, without discerning the words—it had sounded rather like a radio talk show playing quietly behind a closed door—but it must have been that voice that had yanked her so abruptly out of sleep. The drone of traffic seventeen stories down was too ordinary to bother her, the temperature was warm but tolerable, and her bladder wasn't demanding a trip to the bathroom.

A woman who lives alone is never, not even on a sunny Saturday morning, altogether free from fear. A woman who has recently happened upon the murdered body of her next-door neighbor feels even less secure. Martha clearly remembered setting the locks after seeing Melody and Vanessa out. It was an array of locks designed to withstand anything less potent than a battering ram; all the same, for several minutes she lay tensely listening.

Nothing.

The remnants of sleep slipped away. The dream-voice was silent. She decided that her half-awake mind, already disturbed by Arnold's death, must have translated the city noises outside her window into the dream-sound of a voice. To seize the phone and call 911 would be to overreact.

But she should investigate. Maybe there had been a leak in the apartment above, and what she had interpreted as a voice was the drip of water invading her space. If that was what had disturbed her, she must deploy pans and mops and call the super.

She sat up and swung her legs over the side of the bed, fished around with her toes until she located her slippers, slipped her feet into them, and stood up. Her stressed calf muscles threatened to cramp, but a couple of steps loosened them.

Not without a little frisson of trepidation, she ventured out of the bedroom, along the little hall, and into the living room. No one was there, and the front door was properly Yale-locked, Medeco-bolted, and security-chained. She peered into the kitchen. It was tidy and undripped-upon. So was the bathroom. So was her study. Feeling simultaneously anxious and foolish, she opened the door to her study closet. No one had squeezed in among the out-of-season clothes and office supplies.

Of course not; she had only dreamed that voice.

Unsure whether any more sleep was possible but still too tired to face the day, she returned to bed.

And presently, as she drifted once more between waking and sleeping, that half-heard voice began to murmur again. She strained to distinguish words, and all at once she was wide awake and the mental door was wide open and the words were distinct in her ears. She could even hear the voice speaking them. It was John's voice, and the words were those he had spoken the evening before. "Do you have any idea," he had asked, "how hot a wig can get?"

Wig.

That was the word that had invaded her sleep: *wig.*

Everett Upton wore a wig.

Everett Upton's wig was dark and wavy.

She scrambled off the bed, went to the kitchen, put on the kettle, and while it heated, considered Everett Upton and the terrible toupee.

Melody had seen the dark-haired man in the stairwell on a Sunday afternoon. The Uptons were churchgoers, but church was no alibi; church was over by noon.

The Uptons lived on the fifth floor, so if Everett had been on the seventeenth floor, and if he had gone home by way of the stairs, Melody could have seen him going down.

And so what?

Everett could have had a perfectly valid reason for being on the seventeenth floor on that Sunday afternoon. For instance, Arnold Stern and Irene Xendopoulis were friends, and Irene had been taken to the hospital while Arnold was away. Mightn't Everett have come up to the seventeenth floor to tell Arnold?

But Everett disliked Arnold, was jealous of Arnold's friendship with Irene. Why would he bother?

The kettle whistled. She poured the water onto a tea bag in a mug, set the timer, and considered that Everett might have felt an obligation to Irene, if not to Arnold.

But why would Everett bother to come up twelve floors to deliver the news? Why not telephone? And why return home via the stairs rather than the elevator? Martha had never seen any indication that Everett Upton was a fitness fanatic.

The timer beeped. She removed the tea bag from

the mug, poured in a driblet of milk, and took that first hot, stimulating sip.

And remembered that someone had recently said something about Everett Upton.

Paul.

Paul Willard, her host in Phillips Landing. What was it Paul had said? Something about not leaving Everett Upton alone with the family silver.

She wavered for a few minutes, but then she went into her study and got the Rolodex and carried it out to the living room and picked up the phone by the chaise.

"I SHOULDN'T HAVE said that," said Paul.

"But you did," said Martha.

"Then you're supposed to be forgetting it."

"But I'm not."

"Nell will send me to bed without my supper."

"Paul, you started this."

"I shouldn't have. It was just an old piece of gossip. I don't know if it'd be fair to pass it on. It was quite a while ago, and I'm not even sure there's anything in it. I only heard it third-hand, and the guy who told the guy who told me doesn't like Everett."

"Paul."

"Yes, I know. Why did I bring it up in the first place if I wasn't willing to pass it on?"

"Exactly."

"And you're scrambling around in the middle of a murder case, and it's making you crazy."

"That's a fair assessment."

''We can't have that.''

''I agree.''

''Just keep in mind that I'm not guaranteeing there's any truth to the story. There's bad feeling.''

''I shall heed your warning.''

''And I just bet you will. Okay, here it is, and you'll have to admit that it's a little peculiar.''

This was the story:

A good many years ago—Paul wasn't sure how many—Everett Upton had interviewed a dealer in antiquities for an article about some of the dealer's holdings. In the course of the interview, the dealer had been called away to the telephone, leaving Everett alone in the gallery with an unlocked display cabinet. The next day, the dealer's assistant had called her boss's attention to the fact that a small artifact—Paul thought it was an Etruscan body ornament—was no longer in the display cabinet. The dealer hadn't noticed it was gone.

''That seems odd,'' said Martha.

''The word around town is that the old boy was getting past it. Maybe the phone call had distracted him. Anyway, when he realized the little *objet* wasn't there anymore, he called Everett to ask if he remembered seeing it in the display cabinet.''

''A veiled accusation?''

''Apparently not. He just seems to have been trying to pin down how long it had been missing. He and Everett went back a long way, and my informant thinks it didn't even cross his mind that Everett might have had anything to do with the vanishing act. Anyway, I'm told that Everett said he didn't remember whether he'd seen the thing or not.''

''Is that likely?''

''It's possible, I guess. If there was a lot of stuff and that particular item wasn't one of the ones he was writing about, it might not have stuck in his mind. Anyway, Everett offered to come down to the gallery to help look for it, and the dealer said fine, and Everett went down, and lo and behold, there it was, tucked away on a shelf in a little workroom in back of the shop.''

''Odd.''

''It gets odder. The guy who doesn't like Everett told the guy who told me that it was Everett who found it. He and the dealer were on opposite sides of the workroom when Everett yelled 'Eureka.'''

''I see.''

''Yup.''

''And how did the dealer suppose that this wandering artifact had got into the workroom?''

''Well, as I said, he was getting past it. People who don't have any bone to pick with Everett think that the old man must have taken it back there to do some work on it—clean it or label it or something—and forgot he'd left it there. The old boy's dead now, and the shop's a Starbucks or something.''

''Wouldn't the assistant have known?''

''As far as my informant knows, she never contradicted the old man. But what the first guy—the guy who doesn't like Everett—what he thinks is that Everett took the thing, thinking the old man wouldn't miss it for quite a while, if ever. Then when the loss was discovered so soon, Everett arranged to quote-unquote find it, in a place where it might possibly have been in the first place.''

''Was the disappearance reported to the police?''

''It seems not. I suppose since the thing turned up so promptly, the old man didn't want to expose his senior moment to professional investigation.''

''But the story got around.''

''This is the world of arts and antiquities, my friend. The assistant got a new job after the old boy packed it in, and I guess the story was too good to keep to herself.''

''Was Everett's article published?''

''Yes, it was.''

''And he's still getting writing assignments.''

''He's an editor, so he's the one giving out assignments. And to be fair, he's got serious expertise.''

''Which I suppose gives him a substantial amount of benefit of the doubt.''

''You said it; I didn't.''

''Do his interviewees leave him alone with unlocked cabinets these days?''

''Everybody has cell phones these days, so nobody leaves a room to take a call. Anyway, that's what I meant about the family silver, and if Nell sends me to bed without my supper, it'll be your fault. Now when are you going to move up here where you can hear the thrushes sing?''

''I'd miss my concerts.''

''Thrushes are sweeter.''

"I'd have to get a car again."

"Last I heard, Metro-North is planning to stay in business."

"But I'd need a car to get around up there."

"And God forbid you should be like the rest of us."

"That might be it. Paul, thank you very much for passing along the story."

"Well, I hope you aren't going to put old Ev out of commission. He likes my work."

AN ODD STORY. And while Paul was relating it, two more of those confounded submerged memories had begun to surface. They were small events, both of them, one even tinier than those four words—*"Peter, it's all right"*—that Irene had called out as her nephew had been heading back to the elevator.

What Martha now remembered was that after Irene had spoken them, Peter had hesitated for a perceptible moment before he responded. Might that hesitation have meant that Peter hadn't understood what Irene meant? Maybe, while Irene believed Peter had taken the kylix, in fact he hadn't.

The other little memory was of something that had occurred on a Sunday morning several weeks ago, something much like Irene's sending Peter back for something while they were waiting for the ambulance.

Martha had been approaching the building on the way home from breakfast at her favorite diner, and had met the Uptons and Irene coming out the lobby door on their way to church. The morning having proved to be colder than predicted, Irene had given

Everett her keys and sent him back up to her apartment to fetch a coat.

What if, while Everett was in Irene's apartment, he had been overwhelmed with the acquisitive impulse that had driven him to purloin that little artifact from the senile dealer? It was obvious that he was powerfully attracted to the thing. What if, before hurrying back down to the lobby with Irene's coat, he had taken the kylix from its hiding place in her apartment and hidden it in his own apartment?

Suppose, as Martha had already done, that Irene had told Arnold the kylix had disappeared. Suppose that it was Everett, not Peter, whom Arnold had confronted....

Oh, enough of this. These appalling conjectures were supported only by gossip. Fourth-hand hearsay, and defamatory hearsay at that.

Her tea had grown cold. She poured it down the sink and made a fresh mugful.

TWENTY

Minutes

MARTHA COMPLIED WITH that exasperated directive, *enough of this,* by plunging into serious work. On Friday, while she had been over in Brooklyn Heights listening to Mackie McGarrity, one of her client firms had e-mailed a rather intriguing new assignment. She switched on her computer, logged on to Lexis, and began searching for precedents.

By three in the afternoon, she had finished the research and the first half of the first draft of her memo. She got up from her desk to rummage in the refrigerator for a belated lunch. As soon as her mind was freed from legal analysis, it insisted on returning to its former line of—well, of what? It couldn't in good conscience be called reasoning. Sick fantasy was more like it.

So be it. The past week's events were so improbable that it was no wonder her mind was reluctant to dismiss any hypothesis, however fantastically unhealthy it might seem to be. While she smeared mayonnaise on two slices of bread and laid a slice of deli roast beef between them, she gave in to the obsession just enough to allow herself to ponder the hypothetical conclusion that, to conceal his hypothetical theft of the kylix, Everett Upton had shot Arnold Stern.

There was a discontinuity in this fantasy. If Arnold had suspected Everett of stealing the kylix, he must have had some reason to suspect him.

Could Arnold have known about that old story Paul had just told her? Lila collected art ceramics, so possibly she was aware of art world gossip and, in happier times, had passed the tale on to Arnold.

But if Arnold had heard that defamatory rumor, wouldn't he have told the board that he had doubts about the Uptons' suitability when they had applied for admittance to the building? And if the board had known, would it have approved the Uptons' purchase?

There might be an answer in the minutes of the board meeting at which the Uptons had been approved.

The Uptons had moved into the building seven years ago. Martha remembered the day only too well: August thirteenth, the day of Edwin's first heart attack. When the ambulance arrived at the service entrance, the moving van was blocking the alleyway and the movers were monopolizing the freight elevator. The ambulance had to drive around the block to the front of the building so the EMTs could use a passenger elevator. The delay had driven Martha frantic.

The relevant board meeting would have occurred a few months before.

But today was Sunday; no one would be in the managing agent's office.

RASHIDA GRANT answered the phone on Monday morning. Yes, they had minutes on file, and shareholders were entitled to look at them. Seven years ago? Probably early in the year? No problem. If Ms. Patterson came in between nine and five, she could take a look. After lunch would be best. Two-thirty okay?

THE OFFICE WAS half way up the Chrysler Building, high above the intersection of Forty-second Street and Lexington Avenue. Grand Central was right next door, and the subway made a straight run to it, but Martha opted to walk. The distance was a little less than two miles, and city sidewalks were easier on the knees than rocky trails, and exercise might dispel that annoying headache.

But as she strode steadily up lower Park Avenue, she began to doubt the efficacy of this exercise. It had been a long time since she had noticed how full Manhattan streets were of exhaust fumes and traffic noise. Mountain air and thrush song must have sharpened her awareness. Maybe, she thought, only half frivolously, she should reconsider Paul Willard's suggestion.

THE CARPET IN the reception area was industrial no-color. (Some residue from the discussion with Mackie McGarrity was causing her to notice carpets.) The institutional-cream walls were finger-smudged around the light switches. The air-conditioning was frigid.

Rashida Grant sat behind a desk facing the outer

door. The "How're you doing?" with which she greeted Martha sounded like a genuine inquiry.

"Reasonably well," Martha said. "And you?"

"Getting there. I didn't have any nightmares the last couple of nights, so maybe that's over and done with. Don't know if I'll ever be able to deal with steak again, though, know what I mean?"

"I'm afraid I do," said Martha.

"Do they know who did it? Like, have a suspect? The TV isn't saying."

"Not as far as I know."

"Does this thing with the minutes have anything to do with it?"

"If you don't mind, I don't think I'd better say. I don't want to run the risk of slandering somebody."

"Right. I know what you mean. Well, I think I found what you want." Rashida picked up two loose-leaf binders from the desk and got to her feet. "Come on back and see if these do the job."

As they passed through a door behind her desk into a short corridor, she said, "I wish I didn't keep remembering him like that, the way we found him. He was a good man, friendly, you know. Acted like he cared about who you were, not just what you were doing for him."

Flirting?

"Did the briefcase ever show up?" Martha asked.

"The thing that got us into all the trouble? I heard they found it in that bedroom."

"Did it have the papers you wanted?"

"I didn't ask, but Mr. Palladino stopped fussing, so

I guess it worked out. Me, I don't want to have anything to do with any of it, ever again. I thought about changing jobs. Problem is, if I change jobs, I lose benefits.'' She turned into a windowless conference room, switched on the overhead light, and laid the binders on the fake-wood tabletop. ''Nobody's going to bother you here. Anything you need, I'm right out front. How about some coffee?''

''Thanks, I will,'' said Martha.

THE COFFEE was hot, bitter, and tasted of plastic foam. By the time she found and read the entry, Martha had consumed half a cup of it and had also concluded that the results of her search were hardly worth the trip. According to the minutes, the admissions committee had reported favorably on the Uptons' application, Yolanda Young had moved to approve, and the motion had passed unanimously. No discussion was recorded, and Arnold Stern was not recorded as having said anything of substance.

Talking with someone who had been there would evidently be the only way to learn whether anyone had, in fact, said anything of substance. Martha checked the attendance list. Helen Taubensee, her first choice, hadn't been a member of the board seven years ago. The only other board member Martha was personally acquainted with was Yolanda Young.

She took the binders back to Rashida and thanked her for her help. The frigidity of the air-conditioning had revived the aches in her legs, so she took the subway home.

TWENTY-ONE

Yolanda

WELL, ALMOST HOME. The Lexington Avenue local carried her as far as Astor Place, leaving her with a three-block walk to her building. The route led past the ice-cream shop where she had met Vanessa and the children. Today ice cream did not tempt her, but this unremarkable element of the Greenwich Village street scene summoned another trivial episode from the shadowy closet in the back of her mind, from which memories kept popping out like clowns from an old Volkswagen Beetle. Its appearance at this moment when she was occupied with questions about Everett Upton invested it with a (possibly spurious) air of significance.

While she had been trying to eat an ice-cream cone with decorum while exchanging neighborly remarks with Vanessa, those crafty little conspirators, Melody Callaghan and Tyler Kaplowitz, had been standing next to the subway-stop railing looking down through the uprights at the heads of the passengers coming up the stairs. Everett Upton had been one of the detraining passengers, and as soon as he appeared, Melody had scurried over to her mother and demanded to be taken home.

Had Melody, looking down on the top of Everett's head, recognized that dark wavy hairpiece?

MARTHA LET HERSELF into her apartment and bolted the door behind her.

Yolanda Young might remember if anything unrecorded had been said at the board meeting. But Yolanda Young had disappeared. In any case, having recently listened to Mackie McGarrity's story about carpet and granite, Martha was not inclined to ask Yolanda Young anything at all about co-op affairs. *Let it be,* she ordered herself. The memorandum she had started yesterday was finished and ready for proofreading.

A LITTLE MORE THAN half an hour later, she had completed the proofreading, entered the corrections, saved the product on a disk, printed out a hard copy for her own files, and sent the memorandum and her bill through cyberspace—and had thereby freed her mind to conjure up second thoughts without restraint.

After all, where was the risk in talking to Yolanda Young about Everett Upton? Everett Upton had nothing to do with carpets and countertops.

But Yolanda had disappeared.

Still, that news was several days old. Might she have returned?

Boris would know.

It was now five-fifteen. Boris came on duty at six.

Martha found an hour's worth of fiddly housekeeping tasks with which to stall, and at six-fifteen went back to the chaise and called down to the doorman's podium.

Yes, Boris said, Ms. Young was at home; he had just seen her come in. Martha asked for her telephone number; Boris read it to her.

She tried to banish carpets and granite countertops from the forefront of her mind while she punched in the number. A taped message answered. Before Martha had finished dictating her number, Yolanda picked up. "Sorry," she said. "I've been screening everything since—you know."

"I understand," said Martha. "If you have a few minutes, there's something I'd like to ask you."

"About Arnold?"

"In a way."

"I'm talked out about Arnold."

Martha disregarded the dismissal. "Is that why you went away?" she asked.

"I went away because I was scared away. Someone said I was going to die, and then Arnold died. Don't tell me you'd have hung around to find out if they meant it."

"But you've come back."

"Trust me, I'd rather be on the space station, but we've got a big project coming up at work, and if I screw up, I'm history. So, all right, what do you want to know?"

"It's a little complicated for the telephone," said Martha. "Would you mind if I came down?"

A pause.

"Or," Martha added, "would it be easier for you to come up here?"

"Forget that. No way am I about to come up to that floor. Oh, the hell with it. Come on down."

AGAIN MARTHA SAT on the leather sofa; again Yolanda offered coffee. This time Martha declined; half a cup of Rashida Grant's brew had carried enough jolt to serve a tea-drinker for a week.

Hoping her scrutiny wasn't obvious, Martha stared at the floor at her feet while Yolanda made coffee for herself. The color of the carpet was neutral—it would probably be called taupe—with a darker sort of mottling that would be good at concealing dirt and wear. It did, as far as she could recall, resemble the new carpet down in the lobby, but she would need to compare samples to tell if they were identical.

Yolanda brought her own coffee to the granite-topped serving bar, perched on one of the leather-topped bar stools, and said, "Okay, what's this about?"

Martha reserved thoughts of carpet and granite for later consideration, transferred her gaze from the floor to her hostess, and said, "A confidential question."

"About Arnold?"

"Maybe. It depends on the answer."

"That's a big help."

It would be imprudent to say that her intention was less to help than to be helped. Martha held her tongue and let the silence grow.

After a moment, Yolanda said, "Okay, confidential."

"Thank you. It has to do with the Uptons."

"Who? Oh, the Brit with the bad rug and the loony wife. What about them?"

"When the board was considering their application, did Arnold express any reservations about their suitability as shareholders?"

"What kind of reservations?"

"Anything related to their suitability."

"That takes in a lot of territory. Dogs, kids, bongo drums, finances."

"I know."

"I don't remember. It was years ago. If there was anything, it couldn't have been serious, because we let them in."

"So Arnold didn't have a problem with their application?"

"I wish you'd be more specific."

"I don't want to defame a neighbor."

A puff of breath might have been an aborted laugh. "You're close already, aren't you?"

"Not really. A question isn't a statement."

"God, lawyers." Yolanda raised her cup to drink. "No, wait." She set it down with a click. "There was something. It didn't come up at the board meeting, Arnold mentioned it to me privately. It was after they were in."

"What was it?"

"Nothing, really. Just that he'd heard something sort of shady, but it was too late to do anything about it, so he'd better keep it confidential. You're sounding just like him.''

"Do you have any idea what it was?''

"Not a clue. The worst thing I know about him is that hairpiece, and you can't call that confidential. The wife's a little loony, but that wasn't any secret either; we all noticed it.'' Yolanda was silent for a moment. "I don't know where you're going with this,'' she said then, "but I can tell you one thing. He didn't make that phone call. Neither one of them did.''

"You're sure?''

"Positive. She has that whispery voice, and he has that accent. Whoever it was, they spoke right out, and they didn't have any accent. Not even around the edges—you know what I mean? And I never did anything to mess up their life. The only time I had anything to do with that pair was when they applied, and I voted for them. I think I even made the motion.'' Yolanda drained her coffee cup. "And talking about messing up people's lives, what about that little girl with the turkey-baster pregnancy and her butch girlfriend with the stupid name? What is it she calls herself, Butterfly?''

"Bird.''

"It ought to be Horse, the way she's built. They submitted this awful renovation plan, and when the board said it wouldn't do, they pitched a fit. Said we were messing up their lives. Those actual words: 'messing up our lives.' That's what that mystery caller said. 'Stop messing up people's lives.'''

"The plan was bad?''

"Unbelievable. I'd like to know what planet their architect's from. They wanted to partition a barely adequate bedroom to make two squeezed little rooms. Truly unlivable. And their so-called plan for the plumbing was so weird, I can't even remember what it was. I ask you, how does it work out that I'm messing up their lives when they're the ones who started this baby without having a place to put it? I mean, it isn't as if the girl could get pregnant by accident."

Martha said nothing.

Yolanda emitted another chopped-off laugh. "Politically incorrect?" she said. "Okay, how about Jeff the mouth and his wife the stalker? They're hetero enough."

Startled into speech, Martha said, "Stalker?"

"You live next door and you don't know? I don't see how you missed it. She had such a crush on Arnold, it was pathetic. He couldn't go out without finding her in the elevator. I mean, okay, it happens when you live in the same wing, but every time he went out? He decided she must be listening to him walking around—they live right under him—and when she heard him going out the door, she'd run out and call the elevator after it went up past her floor, so it'd stop for her on the way down when he'd be in it. You know what I'm saying?"

Martha knew what she was saying. If this conjecture was true, Melody might well have learned deviousness at home.

"You should have heard her when we turned down their buyers," Yolanda said. "Jeff's the one who wants to sell and move uptown. She doesn't want to sell, she *lo-o-oves* the Village. You know how stalkers think everything is about them? After we disapproved the sale, she was all over Arnold, like he'd done it just for her. He thought it started when they applied to buy in. He asked one of his standard questions, why did they want to live here, and she gushed about how she just *l-o-o-oves* the Village, and he said something polite like 'I know what you mean,' and she decided they were kindred spirits.''

Polite? Maybe. Or maybe Arnold's manner had gone beyond polite and approached what Lila called *flirting*.

''Maybe Jeff the Mouth caught on,'' Yolanda said. ''Maybe she did it once too often, and he went up to Arnold's to make a stink and things got out of hand.''

Maybe this, maybe that. Perhaps turning the sudden and violent death of a friend into a guessing game was Yolanda's way of coping with the loss. Martha doubted that her own conjectures were any more defensible. She suppressed an annoyed sigh and gathered herself to leave.

TWENTY-TWO

The Uptons

BACK AT HOME, the door locked and bolted behind her, Martha settled on the chaise and took up *Emma*. After a quarter of an hour's struggle to focus, she closed the book. Jane Austen's familiar felicities had lost their power to shut out current preoccupations. Somewhere, never far below the level of consciousness, lurked the disquieting awareness that on the other side of these enclosing walls someone had shot her neighbor.

Maybe it was time to move. Maybe this apartment—this space that had been her home since Robert was a newborn—was no longer a good place to be. Maybe she really should consider Paul Willard's urging more seriously. Cyberspace rendered geography meaningless; she could do her work as efficiently in the Hudson Highlands as in the city.

She rotated her head to loosen a tightness in her neck and wondered if the prospect of leaving this familiar space was frightening her. But Martha Jenkins Patterson had never been much frightened by stepping into the unknown; something other than fear must be at work. She looked at her watch and saw that it was after six. Very likely it was hunger that was troubling her.

She went out to her favorite Chinese restaurant. The waiter knew her name. This was her village.

THE PHONE RANG not long after she got home. Hoping that one of her friends had obtained tickets to some sort of obscure but amusing performance in one of the outer boroughs, she lifted the receiver and said, "Martha Patterson speaking."

And heard, in the unmistakable tones of the British Isles, "A-a-ah, yes. Everett Upton here."

Startled, she had the momentary illusion that her preoccupation with Everett and the kylix had somehow conjured up this call. And Yolanda Young had made an excellent point; Everett Upton would be incapable of placing an anonymous telephone call to anyone who had already heard him speak.

"I, a-ah, hope I'm not troubling you," he said.

Martha gathered her wits and said, "No trouble at all."

"Kind of you," he said. "The fact is, I have a somewhat, a-a-ah, bizarre request. If it isn't too much of a bother, I wonder if I might come up and have a bit of a chat with you."

Surprise gave way to curiosity; within seconds, curiosity had to contend with a quiver of apprehension.

"At your convenience," Everett added.

Curiosity won. "Now," she said, "would be perfectly convenient."

SHE HUNG UP, considered whether to offer him tea, and decided against that little gesture of hospitality. Apprehension, somewhat shamed but not altogether banished, pointed out that providing tea without visiting the kitchen was impossible, and that the kitchen, with only one means of exit, was a potential trap. She made a further concession to paranoia by slightly rearranging the living-room furniture to place the chair she proposed to offer Everett farther from the front door than the one in which she proposed to sit.

Absurd, of course. But someone—possibly someone with dark wavy hair—had shot Arnold Stern.

WHEN EVERETT ARRIVED, the precautions seemed even more absurd. Even wearing that dark wavy hairpiece, Everett Upton in the flesh was far less threatening than the Everett Upton of her ungoverned apprehension. He took the offered chair; she sat where she had planned to sit; he *a-a-ah*ed a few more times and at last came to the point.

It was about the kylix. "The police got hold of it some way," he said.

"I turned it over to them," she said.

"That—a-a-ah—was prudent of you, I'm sure. Yes. Well. If you don't mind my asking, have they taken your fingerprints?"

"Yes."

"They took mine, as well. It seemed a bit...well, that's neither here nor there. It seems that when they examined the pot they found my fingerprints on it, and they wanted to know how they had got there. I told them you had asked me to, so to speak, validate its provenance, and that, of course, entailed my handling it a good bit."

"Yes, I see."

"Perhaps I'm being a bit irrational—" a little bark of embarrassed laughter "—but this situation is quite out of my experience."

"Just so."

"They didn't appear precisely skeptical, but they do, after all, have the police mentality. Under the circumstances, I decided it would be prudent to apprise you of the situation and assure myself that you'd confirm what I'd told them."

"That you handled the kylix in my presence? And at my request?"

"A-a-ah, yes. Precisely."

"Of course."

"I should appreciate it greatly."

"It's no more than the simple truth. Would you like me to take the initiative in bringing it up, or should I wait for the police to ask me?"

"I suppose… Well, in a situation like this, it's hard to know what's best, isn't it? On the one hand, I shouldn't want to appear anxious, but on the other hand—perhaps…"

"I'll call Detective White."

"I think perhaps that would be best."

SHE OFFERED HIM tea, after all. He declined. Having learned on a long-ago trip to London that English coffee was undrinkable, she suspected that an Englishman might find American tea equally nasty.

As soon as he had left, she dug out Detective White's card and dialed. He was at his desk. He listened and allowed her to feel that her information might be of some importance by asking her to repeat the date and time when Everett had examined the kylix.

THE NIGHT WAS muggy; the morning was worse. Martha rose from the sticky sheets, dressed as scantily as was decent, and set to work on a new assignment that had just come in.

In midmorning, the telephone rang, and when she answered she heard a whispery voice say, "This is Fiona Upton. Everett's wife? I must apologize for troubling you."

Astonishment overrode absolute honesty; Martha said, "Not at all."

"You're kind. I believe…" The rustle of an indrawn breath came across the line, followed by a louder rustle as it was let out. "I believe my husband spoke with you yesterday evening?"

Now what? "Yes, he did."

"I wonder… Please don't think I'm…I need to talk with you. If it isn't too much trouble—would now be convenient?"

Martha's current deadline was several days away. "Yes," she said.

"Thank you so much. And would you be able to

come down here? I wouldn't trouble you, but I'm not well and I find it hard to go out on my own.''

Martha took a moment to devise a prudent course of action; then she said, ''Yes, if you like. I'll be there in a few minutes.''

SHE SLUNG HER handbag over her shoulder and took the elevator to the lobby. The weekday doorman was in his shirtsleeves, and his shirtsleeves were rolled above his elbows.

''Still hot,'' Martha said.

''They fix it, it bust again.''

''Annoying. I need your help.''

''Whatever I can do.''

''Thank you. I've been invited to visit the Uptons, and I was in the elevator before I realized that I don't know their apartment number. Could you help me out? Everett Upton.''

''Sure, no problem.'' He riffled through a stapled set of pages, ran his finger down a list, and said, ''Upton. Five A.''

''Thank you. I'm going there now.''

FIONA UPTON WAS tall, big boned, and long jawed, with indeterminate-colored hair in a straggly bun. Tweeds would suit her, but today tweeds would be intolerable; she was wearing a plain tan dress that delivered the same message. Only an anxious furrow between her eyebrows marred the image of a horsy middle-class countrywoman. Unwell she might claim to be, but except for those anxiety lines, she looked healthy enough.

She indicated a chair and said in that tentative, whispery voice, "Isn't this heat frightful?"

Martha settled into the chair and delivered the speech she had prepared before leaving home. "I think it's addling my brains," she said. "It wasn't until I was in the elevator that I realized I don't know your apartment number, so I had to go down to the lobby and ask the doorman." Thus, in spite of feeling foolish, she let Fiona Upton know that someone knew where she was.

Fiona sat down in another chair and plunged into speech as if taking a header off a high board. "When my husband spoke with you yesterday," she said, "what did he want to talk about?"

Everett had not asked for confidentiality. Martha said, "A Greek pot."

Fiona's hands sketched the kylix's shape in the air. "A sort of saucer with handles, attached to a base?"

"Yes. He called it a kylix."

"Did he say anything more about it?"

"He said the police were asking why his fingerprints were on it. I'd asked him about it earlier, so he wanted me to confirm that he had handled it when I'd shown it to him."

"How—oh, please forgive me if I seem rude, but I need to know. How did you come to have this pot?"

"Lila Stern found it in the apartment after Arnold died. She told me she didn't know how it had got there, but since it appeared to be Greek, she thought it might belong to Irene Xendopoulis. The apartment is unoccupied, so I took it for safekeeping, and later I asked your husband to look at it and identify it if he could. He confirmed that it was Irene's. Since she was incommunicado in the hospital, and no one else could explain why it had turned up in the Sterns' apartment, I turned it over to the police.''

"I see.'' Fiona fiddled with the collar of her dress, patted a wisp of hair into place, clasped her hands in her lap, and stared at the floor. "The detective came here. It was quite disturbing.'' She looked up. "I suppose you should know,'' she said. "I took that pot from Ms. Xendopoulis's apartment.''

TWENTY-THREE

The Kylix Again

THE SILENCE might have lasted two seconds or it might have lasted ten.

"How?" Martha asked at last. "When?"

"I don't remember." Fiona's voice grew even softer. "It was a Sunday, but I can't remember which one. We were picking her up to take her to church. When she had trouble getting around, Everett liked to help. She attends a Greek Orthodox church on Seventeenth Street, and we go to Saint John the Divine up on a Hundred and Tenth, so it is really not at all out of our way."

Martha tried to suppress her impatience with the geographical digression. "What happened?" she prompted.

"Oh. Yes." Fiona raised her hands to her face and scrubbed her cheeks with her palms. "That's why I asked you here. To tell you what happened. Yes. Well, we were in her apartment, picking her up to take her to church, as we always did, and I had to go to the bathroom." Again that odd scrubbing of her cheeks. "On the way past her bedroom, I glanced through the door, and I saw it in there. That pot. On a shelf in her bedroom. I don't know what I was thinking. On the way back, I slipped into her room and picked it up and put it in my bag.''

In her *bag*? What kind of bag did this woman carry to church? The kylix was at least six inches high, and easily eight or nine inches across from handle to handle. It would take a satchel the size of a shopping bag to accommodate it. Not to mention the risk of breakage.

Martha's face must have expressed her doubt, for again Fiona's hands sketched a shape in the air: a sizable rectangle, perhaps eighteen by twenty-four inches. ''It's a large bag,'' she said. She added, ''I took off my scarf and wrapped it up, to protect it.''

''And you took it to church with you?''

''I don't know what I was thinking.'' Again Fiona scrubbed her cheeks. ''When we got home, I put it in the back of my lingerie drawer.''

''Why?''

''To hide it.''

''No, I mean why did you take it?''

''I don't know. I just don't know what I was thinking.''

''Did your husband know you'd taken it?''

''He never mentioned it.''

''Did Irene say anything about its being missing?''

''Not to me.''

''To your husband?''

''He never mentioned it.''

Silence hovered. "What happened then?" Martha asked at last.

"Happened?"

"It was found in Arnold Stern's apartment, so something more must have happened."

"Oh." Fiona dropped her hands into her lap. Staring down at them, she said, "It's such a terrible story. Years ago, some of Everett's enemies began to circulate a rumor." She looked up. "He has enemies, you know. Anyone who becomes an expert in any field is bound to make enemies, just by being an expert. By being in a position to show how little others know. It was only a rumor, a scurrilous, slanderous rumor. There wasn't a grain of truth in it. A senile old dealer misplaced something in his shop, and some hateful people claimed that Everett had taken it. The thing was found right there in the shop, but they wouldn't let the story die. Nobody believed it, nobody that mattered, just a handful of people who were jealous of his standing in his field. But it wouldn't die. It just wouldn't die."

"And—?" prodded Martha.

"Mr. Stern heard it somewhere. Irene—Ms. Xendopoulis—told him the pot was missing, and he came storming down here, accusing Everett."

An inappropriate smile of triumph threatened to break through Martha's investigative facade; one of her obsessive imaginings was not so far from the truth after all. "When was that?" she asked.

"That Sunday."

"Which Sunday?"

"The day...the day he was—"

"The day Arnold Stern was killed?"

"Yes."

"What happened?"

She could barely hear Fiona's whisper: "He accused Everett. He had heard that terrible old story, and he came down to our apartment and accused Everett of being a thief."

"What did your husband say?"

"He had nothing to do with it."

"He denied it?"

"He had nothing to do with it. I was the one who had taken it."

"Did you say anything?"

"I wasn't there. I wasn't in the room. I was in the bedroom."

"But you could hear?"

"The door was open a little."

"So Arnold and your husband were here in the living room, you were in the bedroom, the kylix was in your underwear drawer, and the door was open a bit. That was the situation?"

Fiona nodded.

"So how did Irene Xendopoulis's kylix get from your underwear drawer to Arnold Stern's apartment?"

"Everett gave it to him."

"To Arnold."

Another nod.

"How did he get it to give to him? Did he come into the bedroom, or did you take it out to the living room?"

"He came in. I couldn't move. I was so terrified. He came into the bedroom and got it."

"So he must have known you had it."

"I...yes, I suppose he did. He must have, mustn't he, to know where to find it."

"How did he explain having it. To Arnold?"

"He said... He's very protective of me. He told Mr. Stern that Ms. Xendopoulis had asked us to keep it for her while she was in the hospital."

"Did Mr. Stern accept that explanation?"

"He was very rude."

"So he didn't believe the story."

"I don't think so. He was very rude."

"What happened then?"

"He left. He took it and left. I was so frightened. If anyone found out—that old story was still alive, it just wouldn't die—if anyone found out about this new accusation—it was Everett's livelihood. Our livelihood."

"Was your husband angry with you?"

"He...he was upset. He said he had to go out for a walk. When he's upset, he walks, to calm himself down. He went out, and I was so frightened. So frightened."

"Were you afraid he was going to do something violent?"

"Oh, no. No, of course not. He's a very gentle man. He went out, and I knew I had to talk to Mr. Stern. To tell him it wasn't Everett. Tell him Everett had nothing to do with it. If the story got around, if Mr. Stern told people Everett had taken something again, they'd start believing that old story and we'd be ruined. I had to tell him it wasn't Everett. I knew I had to, but it was so hard. I don't go out...you know?''

Martha was not unsympathetic to those afflicted with phobias. She herself was far from agoraphobic, but she did have trouble with unguarded heights. She nodded.

"I made myself do it," Fiona said. "As soon as Everett left, I made myself go out and call the elevator. And it came, and I got in and rode up to his floor."

Another little silence.

Once more Martha prodded. "What happened?"

"Nothing."

"Didn't you talk to him?"

"I never left the elevator. It's closed in, you see, so it's safe. But when I got to his floor and it was time to go out into the hall, I thought I would faint. They taught me breathing exercises at the clinic, but they didn't help. Well, they helped a little. I didn't faint. But I couldn't leave the elevator. I'd already gone farther alone than I had done for a long time, but I couldn't go any farther. When I looked out, I felt as if my head was spinning, and then I saw someone at his door and I turned back."

Martha's alertness ratcheted up. "Someone was at Arnold's door?"

Fiona nodded.

"Who was it?"

"I don't know. I only saw her back. The door was open a little bit, and she was talking to him through the crack. I was so glad she was there. It was an excuse to come back home.''

''It was a woman?''

''Oh, yes.''

''Do you know if she went in?''

''I don't know. I didn't stay.''

''You said she was talking to Arnold. Did you see him?''

''Well...I saw someone. Someone was there, inside the door, but now that you ask, it was only open a crack and I couldn't really see who it was. I think the chain was on.''

''Did you hear him talking?''

''Just his voice, not what he was saying.''

''Was it Arnold's voice?''

''Oh, yes.'' A pause. ''I think so.'' Another pause. ''But... Well, I may just think it was because it was his apartment. You understand? It was a man's voice, but now that you're asking, that's all I can really say. I was only there a little while, just a few seconds, really, and then I came back home.''

''So you can't say for sure if it was Arnold Stern on the other side of the door.''

''I never gave it a thought. I just assumed it was.''

Dead end.

''What time was it?'' asked Martha.

''What time?'' Fiona looked bewildered. ''I really don't know. I didn't look at my watch.''

That, at least, was probably true. Unless an appointment is impending, a plane to catch, something time-dependent like that, one doesn't look at one's watch.

But there are many paths to information. "What time does your church service end?" Martha asked.

Fiona looked bewildered. "Twelve o'clock," she said.

"What did you do after church?"

"We came home, and I prepared lunch, and we ate, and I washed the dishes."

"That took another hour and a half, perhaps? Maybe two hours?"

"I suppose so."

"So we're now in the vicinity of one-thirty or two."

"I suppose so."

"How much longer was it after that when Arnold Stern came to your apartment?"

"I don't know."

"Estimate?"

Fiona shook her head with the first display of spirit she had shown. "Really, I can't tell you. I lay down for a nap after I finished the dishes. I woke up when he raised his voice, but I didn't look at the clock."

Another dead end. Martha shifted to a new route. "Can you think of anything that might identify the woman you saw at Arnold Stern's door?"

Fiona shook her head. "I know very few people in the building. And I only saw her from the back."

"How tall would you say she was?"

"I really can't say."

"You could tell her height from the back, I should think."

"I didn't really notice. About average, I suppose."

"And her build? Heavy, thin, or average?"

"Not heavy. Not heavy at all. Very slim and trim, actually."

"What was she wearing?"

"I'm sorry, I don't remember. You must realize, I was in a panic state."

"I don't mean to be unsympathetic, it's just that anything might help. For instance, was she wearing a skirt or pants?"

"Oh! Oh, thank you! Yes, she was wearing a skirt. Oh, I should have remembered that, it was so bright, with big bright-pink flowers. And a bright-pink blouse— well, not really a blouse, one of those tops with the narrow straps and no sleeves. It wasn't really a hot day, not nearly as bad as it had been, but she had such pretty arms to show off."

"How about her hair?"

"Yes, I do remember her hair. Oh, it's all coming back to me. It was fair, with just a little wave, hanging down to her shoulders. Pretty, pretty hair."

TWENTY-FOUR

Testing

SOMEONE WAS LYING.

More than one someone was lying.

What if everyone was lying?

Martha returned to her own apartment, picked up the briefcase that had accompanied her into retirement, went out again, and took the elevator down to the second floor. On the way, she examined her belief that Fiona Upton was lying.

It began with *Why?* What conceivable reason could Fiona Upton have had for stealing Irene Xendopoulis's kylix?

But as soon as Martha put the question to herself, she realized that pursuing the *why* wasn't worth the effort. Fiona's reason need not be one that Martha would find rational. For instance, what if Fiona felt that Irene's friendship with Everett amounted to theft of Everett's attention, and that stealing Irene's kylix was just recompense?

Crazy, but perhaps possible.

But even if one set aside the question of why,

Fiona's story was full of other contradictions and improbabilities.

Item: Fiona said she had seen the kylix from the bedroom door, but Irene said she had hidden the pot. Had hidden it from herself, so surely from anyone else who might glance casually through a door.

Item: Would anyone, however irrationally motivated, jam a fragile ceramic pot, even swaddled in a scarf, into a tote bag?

Item: If Fiona had emerged from the back of Irene's apartment with a bulging tote bag that had not previously bulged, wouldn't Irene have noticed the bulge?

Item: If Fiona and Everett had not discussed the theft, how had Everett known where to find the kylix when Arnold came calling?

And last—well, really first—it was Everett, not Fiona, who had a reputation for stealing small artifacts.

Fiona claimed that Everett had gone out for a walk after the confrontation with Arnold. Had Everett actually left the building, or had Everett been the one who went up to Arnold's door?

The elevator stopped, and Martha stepped out on the second floor.

IN SPITE OF the fact that she was entering Irene's apartment at Irene's request, using keys that Irene had lent her for the purpose of entering, to get something Irene had asked her to get, Martha couldn't quite shake the feeling that she should be wearing surgeons' gloves and scanning the ceiling for surveillance cameras.

Once inside, she locked and bolted the door behind her.

A solid, no-nonsense double-pedestal desk stood against the far living-room wall. The left pedestal had two drawers, the lower one double-depth for holding file folders; the right pedestal had three ordinary-size drawers.

Martha laid her handbag and briefcase on top of the desk, pulled out the executive-size swivel chair from the kneehole, and sat down to work. She started with the file drawer in the left pedestal. It was crammed with folders full of professional material, mostly offprints of articles from archaeological journals. Martha stuffed them into her briefcase.

Three of the ordinary-size drawers contained items she was not to concern herself with: pens and pencils, erasers and Wite-Out, stationery and stamps, stapler and staples, rubber bands, Scotch tape, paper clips, floppy disks (some blank, some not), a pocket calculator, a couple of AA batteries. Martha picked the little black stapler out of the clutter, added it to the offprints in her briefcase, and opened the middle drawer on the right. The personal papers Irene wanted were tidily folded into a five-by-ten accordion envelope: Irene's diplomas (B.A., M.A., and Ph.D.), two insurance policies, a copy of her will in an envelope of its own, the stock certificate and the proprietary lease for the apartment, copies of the building's bylaws and house rules. Martha stuffed them into her briefcase next to the offprints, pushed the drawer shut, got to her feet, and found that, with this mission accomplished, her mind was insisting on returning to the latest conundrum.

What if Fiona *hadn't* been lying?

What if some of those apparent contradictions and inconsistencies had credible explanations?

For instance, take the matter of Everett's having known where to find the kylix. Wasn't it possible that he had already come across it in Fiona's drawer before Arnold came calling, and for reasons best known to himself, hadn't mentioned it to Fiona? Who knew how that strange alliance functioned?

As for the contradiction between Fiona's claim that she had seen the kylix in Irene's bedroom and Irene's assertion that she had hidden the thing—wasn't it possible that Irene might recently have been taken with a desire to display it, after all? She hadn't mentioned that when she was discussing the thing with Martha, but illness might driven it out of her memory.

Perhaps that assertion of Fiona's could be checked. Martha got to her feet, headed back toward the bathroom, stopped in front of the bedroom door, and peered in.

Fiona said she had seen the kylix on a shelf. From the doorway, Martha could see no shelf. The only horizontal surface visible from the doorway was the top of a nightstand beside the bed. That surface was barely large enough to hold a lamp, a clock radio, and a tissue box; there was no room on it for anything the size of the kylix. Even if one regarded the tissue box as temporary, the space it occupied still wouldn't safely accommodate that problematic pot.

Martha ventured farther into the bedroom and found it as she remembered it. The bureau top was the only other space that might be termed a shelf, and its clutter of photographs and memorabilia left no room for anything the size of the kylix.

Martha tried to conjure up an explanation that would reconcile the contradiction. If that pot had once been on the bureau, Irene *might* have added objects to the clutter after it disappeared, filling the space it had vacated. But Fiona said she had seen the kylix from the doorway, and the bureau top wasn't visible from the doorway.

If Fiona Upton had stolen the kylix, she hadn't stolen it in the way that she had described.

She probably hadn't stolen it at all. Martha would have given heavy odds that it was Everett who had experienced, and yielded to, that inexplicable irresistible impulse.

What a pair: a kleptomaniac married to an agoraphobe.

(No, that wasn't quite right: kleptomania, she seemed to recall, was the compulsion to steal objects of little value. Everett, apparently, was drawn to things of great value. The family silver.)

Martha went back to the living room, picked up her handbag and briefcase, double-locked the door, went home, and made tea.

Why had Fiona lied?

Probably to protect herself by protecting Everett. For if Everett were arrested, convicted, and impris-

oned, he would no longer be available to escort her
here and there, to blunt the panic she felt in public
spaces; if Everett were imprisoned, Fiona would be
imprisoned as well. If, on the other hand, Fiona took
the blame, she would be the one subject to prosecution; and perhaps the confinement of prison would not
seem as threatening to an agoraphobe as to someone
with a more normal psychic makeup.

But that hypothesis raised another problem: Why
would Fiona suppose that Everett would stand by and
let her assume the blame?

Well, what if Fiona had just now made up that story,
invented it on the spur of the moment without time to
stop and consider how Everett would react if he heard
her taking the blame for his theft?

No, on balance, Fiona's claim to have stolen the
kylix was just not credible.

But what about the second part of the story—the
part about going up to Arnold's apartment? Wasn't it
far more likely that Everett had been the one to make
that little expedition?

Not necessarily. Fiona's account of her journey to
the seventeenth floor, her panic attack and her retreat,
had been a good deal more convincing than her tale
of stealing the kylix. And her description of the clothes
the woman at Arnold's door had been wearing, the
skirt with the hot-pink flowers and the matching tank
top—those clothes existed in the real world; Martha
had seen Vanessa Callaghan wearing that skirt. Surely
it was Fiona who had actually made that harrowing

little excursion, and had aborted it when she saw Vanessa talking with Arnold through the cracked-open door.

Furthermore, that part of Fiona's story was consistent with Yolanda Young's assertion that Vanessa had been stalking Arnold.

Martha's mind skittered to Yolanda Young, and into confusion.

How did Mackie McGarrity's kickback story fit with the kylix's wanderings? What about the anonymous death threat, which had not been delivered in an English accent? What about Bird and Nadine's insistence that Yolanda was *messing up their lives?* And how did Jeff Callaghan's favorite phrase, "Shoot them all," fit into this mess?

What about the dark-haired man Melody had seen in the stairwell?

It was at that point in her imaginings that a wholly new hypothesis made Martha catch her breath. What if, to protect her father, devious little Melody Callaghan had invented the man in the stairwell?

Or what if she had seen a man, but his hair had been red, not dark?

Oh, *stop! Somebody* had to be telling the truth.

TWENTY-FIVE

Jeff

AND FOR SEVERAL MINUTES after she got back to her apartment, she did manage to stop. The hard part, as always, was to stay stopped. Like mental mice or cockroaches, doubts and fantasies kept finding cracks through which to invade her thoughts. Fighting them off was a strenuous exercise—a mental exercise, to be sure, but still one that produced a weariness that was close to exhaustion. She was thoroughly fed up with being exhausted.

Without a great deal of hope, she once more tried driving off the vermin by reclining on the chaise with *Emma*. Presently, with no sense of having slept, she woke. As usual, napping had left her with a thickness behind her eyeballs that was just short of a headache.

She struggled to her feet and found that the day had trudged on to a quarter to six. She couldn't remember eating lunch. Five-forty-five was an outrageously early dinner hour, but she must eat something. Her kitchen contained nothing that appealed to her. She would go out.

WHEN SHE GOT DOWN to the lobby, she found to her dismay that Jeff Callaghan was one of a little crowd of home-coming workers waiting for the elevator. Jeff was not wearing a smiley face: his forehead was creased and the corners of his lips were turned down. All things considered, she would have been happier if she had started either earlier or later, and thus missed this encounter.

But she had been brought up with attention to propriety, so when she came face-to-face with Jeff on her way past the bronze screen that had replaced the ficus, she managed a nod and another of those little movements of the lips that she hoped would resemble a neighborly smile.

Jeff responded more vigorously. He put out a restraining hand, then drew it back before it quite touched her arm. "Got a minute?" he said. "I need to talk to you."

She had any number of minutes; whether she wanted to spend them hearing what Jeff wanted to talk about was an open question. She made her standard noncommittal noise.

Jeff chose to take it as assent. He jerked his head to the side and said, "Over here."

Ignoring his demand would generate more trouble than would complying; Martha accompanied him. When they were out of earshot of the people boarding the elevator, he stopped and demanded, "What's going on?" The words were combative, but his voice was more strained than truculent.

She was reasonably sure she knew which particular

going-on he meant, and that, of all possible goings-on, was the one she couldn't in good conscience discuss.

"Going on?" she temporized.

He flapped a hand in an impatient gesture. "With Melody. Something's got her all upset. She keeps waking up with nightmares, but she won't say what's the matter. She hasn't had bad dreams for years. I don't know what to do."

He had nothing on Martha; she, too, was not sure of what to do. She said, "I'm sorry she's troubled."

Again he made that impatient gesture. "She talked to you the other day."

"Yes."

"What about?"

"Why don't you ask her?"

"She won't tell me. She just starts to cry. It's driving me nuts."

Parenthood can do that. Parents need all the help they can get. Martha did wonder, briefly, whether a boot in the rear might not be of more help to Jeff Callaghan than would a violation of his daughter's confidence, but Martha Patterson was first and last a word person. Mounting a bodily assault would be an act so foreign to her character—not to mention her physical capabilities—that the mere contemplation was absurd.

But still, parents need all the help they can get.

A career in the law had taught Martha the uses of equivocation. As though tiptoeing across broken glass, she said, "Do you recall ever telling Melody that she'd be sent to reform school if she misbehaved?"

"What?" Jeff drew back half a step. "Oh, my God, what did she do?"

"Nothing much."

"But...come on, what is it?"

"I promised her I wouldn't tell you."

"Oh, come *on.* She's a little *kid.* I'm her *father.*"

"Just so." Did neither of the adult Callaghans understand that promises are made to be kept? No, that thought was unfair; Vanessa was evidently keeping her vow of silence. "You're her father, and she's afraid you'll punish her," she said.

"But if it isn't—if it's—like you say, if it's nothing much..." Jeff wiped his hand across his mouth and drew in a breath so deep that it must have filled all the seldom-used air sacs at the very bottom of his lungs. He let it out, glanced past Martha's shoulder at a trickle of home-comers passing through the lobby behind her, and then, more quietly than she would have thought possible, said, "She was playing in the stairs again, wasn't she? That's it, isn't it?"

"I promised her I wouldn't tell."

"You didn't tell, I figured it out. If that's what she's afraid of, I won't punish her. I wouldn't ever... Look, I shoot off my mouth sometimes. Melody knows that. She knows I say stuff I don't mean."

"Maybe," Martha said. "But she's a child, and you're her father. There's an imbalance of power."

For a moment, she thought the concept was beyond his comprehension. But then his shoulders sagged; he looked at the floor and muttered, "Yeah."

"I suggest," she ventured, "that you do everything

you can to make your peace with Melody. She has information...."

But Jeff's attention had shifted. The new direction of his gaze and a barely perceptible movement of the air made her aware that someone had come up behind her. She broke off, looked around, and recognized the someone as Irene's nephew, Peter Sanders.

Peter, who had dark wavy hair.

Which was irrelevant. It wasn't Peter who had stolen the kylix, it was Everett. It had to be Everett.

She gathered her wits and said, "Good evening, Peter. Jeff Callaghan, this is Irene Xendopoulis's nephew, Peter Sanders."

Not much concerned with propriety just at that moment, Jeff muttered, "Yeah, hi," looked at his watch, said, "Gotta go," and headed for the elevator.

His departure left Martha wondering guiltily if she had revealed too much. Could one trust Jeff Callaghan's promise to refrain from once more threatening his little girl with an impossible but terrifying punishment?

TWENTY-SIX

Vanessa

PETER IGNORED the abruptness of Jeff's departure, said, "Nice running into you," to Martha, and moved his feet a few inches toward the elevator.

Martha dropped her semi-guilty contemplation of her semi-violation of Melody's confidence. "You're here to make decisions about your aunt's furniture?" she asked.

"I wish it wasn't necessary."

"She's not happy with the move."

"She hates it. Well, if you'll excuse me, I've got to get cracking. There's a lot to look at."

SINCE SHE WANTED nothing more exotic than a club sandwich on whole-wheat toast, Martha headed for Sixth Avenue and the diner where everyone on the staff knew her name.

Her village.

Forty-five minutes later she was back at home, her blood sugar restored and her headache in abeyance. She made a mug of tea—diner tea was as undrinkable as British coffee—and decided to take advantage of the energy spurt by doing her laundry. Before she had left San Francisco, her daughter-in-law had run her clothes through the washer and dryer, but since then her wardrobe had been through a cross-country plane trip and a New York City heat wave.

Martha had once employed a once-a-week housekeeper, but that had been back in the days when she had been a full-time lawyer. Shortly after she had retired, the housekeeper of the day had departed for a full-time job, with better benefits, as a cleaner in a hospital. With more time on her hands than she had had for forty-plus years, and having learned (not altogether willingly) the elements of housework from her mother, Martha had taken on the task of keeping her house in order while she looked for a suitable replacement. She had been surprised to find that she took a perverse satisfaction in the war against squalor. Finally allowing herself to acknowledge that as one aged, one became one's mother, she abandoned the search for a new housekeeper and added dusting and laundering to her retirement schedule.

She changed the sheets on her bed, emptied the hamper, sorted lights from darks, stuffed the dirty laundry and a jar of measured detergent into a blue-and-white-striped laundry bag she had acquired at a charity bazaar, tucked her copy of *Emma* on top of it, and took the service elevator down to the basement.

The concrete corridor and the laundry room were empty, and all twelve washing machines were silent. She unloaded her darks and lights into separate machines, poured in the detergent, fed coins into slots, sat down on the bench, and opened *Emma*. Some trustful people left their laundry to do itself; Martha preferred to remain on guard while the machines did their work.

HER TWO LOADS had just clicked into their final spin cycles when she heard footsteps coming along the corridor. She closed her book and gave her full attention to the doorway. A moment later, she found that some cosmic schedule-maker had decided that this was to be her day for Callaghans; it was Vanessa who came through the door, trundling behind her a shopping cart full of dirty laundry.

Vanessa hesitated in the doorway when she saw Martha; then, obviously deciding to make the best of an iffy situation, she said, "Oh, hi," and came on in.

Martha experienced her own momentary urge to flee. Her last encounter with Vanessa had not been a particularly pleasant one, and since then she had learned more about the woman than she really wished to know.

But it wasn't she who had done anything about which to feel uncomfortable; it wasn't she who had stalked Arnold Stern in the elevator; it wasn't she who had been standing at his door on the day he had been shot. She stayed put and said, "Good evening." And as she made that neighborly noise, she found herself wondering if she might yet again have been indulging in fantasy. Very likely there were as many slim long-haired blondes with flowered skirts in this city as there were men with dark wavy hair.

Vanessa had no more to say than that initial *Oh, hi*. She loaded and started three of the washing machines, sat down on the far end of the bench, and pulled a copy of *Cosmopolitan* from a pocket on the back of her shopping cart.

Content to be ignored, Martha tried to return to *Emma*. But her concentration was shattered. This encounter had stirred up yet another of those annoying fragments of memory that had been destroying her equanimity. It was something Vanessa had said when they were talking about the man in the stairwell. No, not quite; it was something she had said while Martha was purposely *not* talking about the man in the stairwell.

Vanessa had asked if Melody's secret was about Arnold, and Martha had said something on the order of "Maybe," and Vanessa had said—had more or less blurted out—"She knew, didn't she?" And when Martha had asked, "Knew what?" Vanessa had pulled back and said, "Nothing."

Now Martha asked herself again, *Knew what?*

The tension in the back of her neck was going to keep recurring until she had more facts. She said, "I'd like to ask you a question."

Vanessa looked up. Her expression was not especially neighborly; at best it might be called neutral.

Undeterred, Martha said, "When you were asking about my conversation with Melody, you said, 'She knew, didn't she?'"

"I did?"

"Yes. And I'm wondering what you meant."

"I don't remember."

"Might you have meant that she knew you'd gone up to the Sterns' apartment on the afternoon Arnold was shot?"

A long pause; then Vanessa said, "I didn't know there was a law against talking to a friend."

"You were there."

"Just at the door. I didn't go in, I just talked to him at the door. I was just returning a book he loaned me. He didn't even take the door off the chain; he just took it through the crack. He took it and shut the door and I went home. That's all that happened. *Nothing* happened."

It was a long speech to say nothing but *nothing*. "What book was it?" asked Martha.

"I don't remember. No, wait, it wasn't a book. That was another time. I went... I thought someone should warn him that people were plotting to vote him out of office."

"And did you?"

"I tried to tell him, but he didn't seem to care." Grievance sharpened her voice. "I was trying to look out for his interests, but he never even took the door off the chain."

The acerbity in her voice reinforced Martha's inclination to believe her. If Yolanda's accusation was to be believed—and Martha had no overwhelming reason to doubt it—if Arnold had thought Vanessa was stalking him, then he might well have left the door on the chain when he saw who it was that had come ringing his bell.

She tried for one more fact. "Could you tell if anyone else was in the apartment?" she asked.

"I don't...Oh. You mean someone..." Vanessa shook her head. "I don't know. The chain was on, I told you. All I could see was a sliver of his face. Arnold's face."

"You might have heard someone."

"I didn't. Don't you think I'd say if I did?"

"Was this before or after your husband was there?"

"Jeff? It was before. I went up, and a while later, after I came back home, Jeff went up. Everybody in the world knows he went up. He was just trying to find out what we had to do to sell this place. That's all it was about. Everybody in the world heard them talking."

That was not quite true; the Kaplowitzes had not reported hearing *them*. They had heard *Jeff*. No one had reported hearing *Arnold*.

Could—horrible thought—could Jeff have been shouting at Arnold's dead body, making an audible fuss to protect Vanessa, who had already been up there, by conveying the impression that he had found Arnold alive?

No, if Arnold had been dead when Jeff arrived, who would have let Jeff in?

Could the door have been unlocked?

Stop it! "Was anyone else in the apartment when Jeff was there?" Martha asked. It was a stupid question. If anyone else had been there, Jeff would have made much of the fact.

And of course Vanessa shook her head. "If only," she sighed.

TWENTY-SEVEN

The Bequest

YES, *IF ONLY*.

If only someone else had been in Arnold's apartment that afternoon. If only someone else had joined that parade to the seventeenth floor while Martha was away, someone completely *else,* not a neighbor but a stranger, someone Martha didn't know, didn't care two pins about.

So absurd, that parade: Vanessa, Fiona, Jeff, Lila....

And Everett? Not if Fiona was to be believed. *Fiona* and *believe* were not words that associated amicably in Martha's mind, but Martha did believe in the woman's aborted visit to Arnold that Sunday afternoon.

But then she thought, why wish for *anyone* to have been there? Why not wish that no one had gone to Arnold's apartment that afternoon, that none of this had happened, that one could go up to the seventeenth floor right now and ring Arnold's doorbell and...

"So?" Vanessa's voice just missed being a quaver.

Martha hauled her wandering attention back. "So?" she echoed.

Vanessa frowned. "You know what I mean."

"No, I don't."

"Are you going to tell?"

"No, I'm not."

The frown began to smooth out.

"You are," said Martha, and the frown returned.

But before Vanessa had time to answer—if indeed she meant to answer—a quick patter of feet drew the attention of both of them to the corridor.

"Melody Mary Callaghan, don't you go running off from me!" bellowed a male voice.

A child's voice piped, "I'm finding Mommy!" and Melody scampered into the laundry room.

Vanessa must be fond of hot pink; Melody's shorts and T-shirt were the same color as the big flowers in that skirt that Fiona had described.

"Goddammit..."

"Jeff, it's okay!" Vanessa called. "I'm here!"

Jeff appeared in the doorway. Melody sidled over to the bench, and Vanessa slipped an arm around her. From that sanctuary, Melody said, "Oooh, Daddy, language."

Jeff snapped, "Don't you smart-mouth me, young lady," and then he noticed Martha. "Oh," he said.

"Good evening," said Martha.

"Yeah," he said. "Yeah, hi. Sorry, it's just, you know..."

"It's time?" asked Vanessa.

"Quarter to." He glanced at Martha again. "Bowling night," he explained. He leaned over and kissed Vanessa lightly on the lips, and then put a finger under

Melody's chin. Melody drew back, but when Jeff's touch grew more insistent, she let him tilt her face up and peck her on the cheek. "You behave, now," he said, "or Mommy'll put a leash on you." He headed out the door, and his footsteps faded away toward the stairwell.

Melody touched her neck tentatively.

"He doesn't mean a real leash," Vanessa said. "He just means you should stay where I can see you."

Melody eased free of Vanessa's arm. "People shouldn't say things they don't mean," she announced.

She was clutching a ball in one hand. It was the sort of reddish rubber ball that New York City children call a *Spaldeen* and employ in a wide range of street and schoolyard games. Robert had owned a series of such balls; they were high bouncers and tended to lose themselves down storm drains.

Melody backed away from the bench until her back was almost against the farthest washing machine, cried, "Catch!" and feinted throwing the ball to Vanessa.

Vanessa sighed, but she laid her magazine aside and held out her hands.

Melody threw like a girl, all elbows and shoulders; the ball went wide and ricocheted off the end of the bench toward the door.

"Oh, *language,*" she exclaimed. She dashed after it, retrieved it just outside the doorway, and scampered back in. "Stand up!" she commanded.

Vanessa sighed again. "Honey, I'm tired."

Melody stuck out her lower lip.

"Really, really tired."

Melody bounced the ball on the floor two or three times. Then she threw it against the wall beside the door, caught the rebound, and threw it again.

The first of Martha's washing machines clicked off. She got up from the bench to deal with it. The shift in position caused the tea she had drunk after dinner to produce an uncomfortable pressure in her bladder.

She rather thought there was a rest room down here, somewhere around the right-angled turn in the corridor and beyond the storage room, but she had no wish to explore, and was in any case dubious about the wholesomeness of what she might discover if she did.

Her second machine rumbled to a stop. Trying to ignore her insides, she transferred the contents of both washers into the nearest dryer and inserted quarters. Over the renewed rumble, she said to Vanessa, "I need to go up to my apartment for a few minutes. Will you be all right?"

"Yes, go on." Vanessa sounded irritated. "I'm fine."

Martha had just left the laundry room when one of Melody's throws missed the wall beside the doorway. The ball flew past her and bounced off the corridor wall. In spite of her discomfort, Martha managed to smother the rebound in a two-handed catch. She soft-tossed it back to Melody and went on her way, ridiculously gratified to know that those old softball reactions had not altogether atrophied.

SHE WAS IN a hurry, so of course the elevator wasn't waiting in the basement. She summoned it, and before her discomfort became intolerable, heard it humming. Presently it stopped and opened, and Irene's nephew, Peter Sanders, emerged.

She murmured, "Hello again, Peter," sidled hastily past him, and pressed the 17 button.

"Oh, hello," he said. He stopped the door from closing by inserting a foot in its track. Perhaps she should have overcome her qualms and explored the basement facilities.

"Can you help me?" Peter asked. "I'm looking for the storage room. Aunt Irene said she had some things in a locker down here."

She said, "Through that door," pointing, "down the corridor and around the corner."

"Thanks," he said. He removed his foot and the door slid shut.

HASTE CAUSED HER to fumble with her door locks for a few seconds, but the delay was not disastrous. She slammed the door behind her and ran for the bathroom, lifting her skirt and tugging at her panties as she went.

Aaah.

When she emerged, she noticed that the answering machine was blinking. Plenty of time remained before her laundry would be dry, so, comfortable once more, she sat down on the chaise and punched play.

"After what happened," said Irene's recorded voice, "I'm obsessing about my will, so I'm calling for your advice. I don't... Well, would you please just take a couple of minutes to look at it and see if it needs changing? It's with those papers you're supposed to get out of my desk. And for heaven's sake, bill me for the time.''

Irene kept making that offer, but Martha would send no bill. She had been a trusts and estates lawyer for upwards of forty years. The making and remaking of wills had constituted a substantial portion of her work, and she had enjoyed that work. Retirement had not diminished her fascination with testamentary arrangements; she wanted no payment for legitimately satisfying her curiosity while rendering a simple service to a sick neighbor. She went into her study and took the will out of her briefcase.

IN HER TIME, Martha had seen—had even reluctantly drafted—some outrageous wills. This one might not be quite in the top ten, but it would certainly make the top hundred.

The first bequest was a little unexpected but not really unreasonable: Irene was not leaving the kylix to Peter, but to the Metropolitan Museum of Art. A curmudgeon might question whether the Met had any pressing need for another Greek antiquity, but that was not for Irene's legal advisor to judge; when the time came, the Met's acquisitions staff would know how to deal with the thing.

The next bequest, though, raised Martha's eyebrows more than a bit.

To my nephew Peter Xendopoulis, also known as
Peter Sanders, son of my deceased brother Damon Xendopoulis, also known as David Sanders,
I give, bequeath, and devise the sum of five dollars. Because Damon abandoned the family name
and showed himself incapable of wise management by squandering whatever assets managed to
find their way into his possession, our father
chose not to leave to him or his descendants any
of the capital he had accumulated through hard
work and economical habits. Peter has followed
his father's example in both regards. Therefore, I
see no reason to change my father's arrangements.

Well. Martha had assumed that Irene was fond of
Peter. Just the other day she had said, with what
seemed like genuine affection, *"The boy is being a
real trouper."*

She turned to the end of the will and looked at the
date. Irene had executed this will two years ago. On
the answering machine, she had spoken of changing
the will, so maybe Peter's recent attentions had softened her. Maybe increasing his legacy was the change
she was contemplating. Martha couldn't think why
Irene would need legal advice about whether it *needed*
changing in that regard; but Irene was ill, and illness
can render normally competent people uncertain of
their competency.

She read on, and it was the next bequest that tipped
this document over the edge into outrageousness. After

unnecessarily providing for the Met and insultingly failing to provide for Peter, Irene had chosen to leave the remainder of her estate to

> My dear friend and good neighbor, Arnold Stern, whose sympathetic attention and knowledgeable conversation have enriched the troublesome later years of my life. I want to enable him to realize his desire to take part in archaeological digs without neglecting his parental duty.

Outrageous. The kylix to the Met, five dollars to Peter, the remainder to Arnold, so that he could spend a summer or two wielding trowel and sieve. Or engaging in whatever other activity might have taken his fancy; what Irene said she wanted him to do with this bequest was not expressed in terms that bound him to do with it what she wanted him to do with it. In plain English, Arnold wouldn't have had to go on digs to get Irene's money when she died.

Remainders were notorious hotbeds of trouble. Remainders often constituted the bulk of an estate, and Irene's reasonably comfortable lifestyle indicated that this remainder was no exception.

Flirting pays.

Well, if someone hadn't shot Arnold, it *would have* paid. As it was, however, not only was Arnold dead and thus precluded from receiving Irene's money when in due course she died; so were Lila and their children. For the next sentence of this miserable document provided that if Arnold should predecease

Irene, the entire estate (except the kylix, which was in all situations bound for the Met) was to pass to "my nephew, Peter Xendopoulis, also known as Peter Sanders."

In plain English, now that Arnold was dead, Peter was to get it all. Except, of course, the kylix.

This was crazy. What had happened to the malice Irene had expressed earlier in this same will?

A chill trickled down Martha's spine from neck to tailbone.

Someone had assured that Arnold would indeed predecease Irene.

Peter Sanders had been in the building on the afternoon Arnold had been killed. He said he had been fetching clothing for Irene, but Irene didn't need her own clothing in the ICU.

Peter had dark wavy hair.

No. Slow down. Inheriting Irene's money would be a motive for killing Arnold only if Peter knew what was in the will. And surely Irene wouldn't have told him.

Or would telling him be part of the game? Irene, whom Martha had supposed that she knew, was after all an enigma.

Martha wanted nothing more to do with this crazy game. She would return the will to its maker and decline to provide the advice—whether paid or unpaid—that Irene claimed to want. Let someone else deal with that crazy woman's mess.

Meanwhile, the world had not ceased to rotate on its axis, nor had the hands of her watch stopped crawling around the dial. She must return to the basement and retrieve *Emma,* which in her discomfort and haste she had left lying on the bench, and wait for her laundry to be finished.

TWENTY-EIGHT

The Basement

IT WAS WHILE the elevator was carrying her back down to the basement that the realization struck Martha like a punch to the solar plexus.

Peter could have seen that confounded will.

That night, when Irene sent him up to her apartment to fetch something (the list of medications to which she was allergic—not that it mattered), she had told him to look for it in the middle right-hand drawer of her desk. That was the drawer in which Martha had found the will.

It was not a long will, as wills go; he would have had time to read it before returning to the lobby. He had seemed agitated as he came running across the lobby from the elevator. Martha had supposed him to be anxious about Irene.

The elevator stopped, the door opened, and another chill slid down Martha's back.

Peter was in the basement. And so was Melody.

She tried to calm her quivering midsection with rational analysis. Well, yes, they were both in the basement, but did it matter?

It would matter only if Peter had been the man in the stairwell, and then only if he had seen Melody above him in the stairwell, and after that, only if he saw her now and recognized her as the child who had seen him going down the stairs from the seventeenth floor.

Melody was wearing her hot-pink shorts and top. It was a highly visible outfit, and Martha now remembered that it was the same outfit Melody had been wearing when Martha had encountered her, with Ruth and Tyler, on the plaza on that fatal Sunday.

Before the elevator door finished sliding open, Martha was out and pushing through the fire door into the basement corridor. She seldom ran anymore; now she ran, the scratchy beat of her footsteps on the concrete floor punctuating the rumble of the dryers in the laundry room.

VANESSA WAS ALONE in the room, sitting on the bench, engrossed in her magazine.

"Where's Melody?" Martha meant to sound matter-of-fact, but the question emerged as a demand.

Vanessa looked up. "Right out...isn't she right out there? Playing with her ball? She was there a minute ago."

"She isn't there now."

"Oh, Lord, what am I going to do with her? She just won't leave those stairs alone." Vanessa slapped her magazine down on the bench and sprang to her feet, brushed past Martha, and marched back toward the stairwell.

But Peter wouldn't be on the stairs. Peter had been on his way to the storage room, and the storage room was along the corridor in the other direction.

Vanessa didn't know about Peter.

Again Martha ran, her shoe soles scrunch-slapping on the concrete floor. She shouted, "Melody!" as she ran, and heard no answer.

Beyond the right-angle turn, the rumble of the dryers faded to a drone behind her. Ahead, light from the open door of the storage room laid a pale rhomboid on the corridor floor. Again she shouted. Still she heard no answer.

She stopped, breathing hard, in the storage room doorway. In front of her, a passageway extended from the doorway to the back wall. On both sides, ranks of lockers stood at right angles to the passage, each rank separated from the next by a wide aisle. From where she stood in the doorway, she could see the corner of a carton extending into the passageway from one of the aisles. She saw no one; but a dozen people could hide between those ranks of lockers.

She would be grateful for a dozen people.

She listened. Her heart was hammering, and not just from running. Now that her footsteps were stilled, the only other sound was the murmur of the dryers back around the corner.

"Melody!" she shouted.

Nothing.

She ventured a few steps into the room. Then, breathing slowly to quell panic, she moved forward, peering systematically left and right down each crosswise aisle. She found herself tiptoeing and recognized her caution as absurd; anyone who might be in that room already knew she was there.

When she reached the aisle where the carton rested on the floor, she found the door of the first locker standing open. It opened outward, blocking her view down the aisle.

She glanced behind her. The retreat route along the passageway to the corridor was clear. She stepped past the carton into the aisle and peered around the open locker door. Nobody was hiding in the locker, and the aisle beyond it was empty.

She returned to the main passageway and checked the remaining aisles. They were all empty.

She backtracked and again peered into the open locker. A heap of taped-shut cartons filled most of the floor space. A grisly thought flashed across her mind; but she saw at once that they were all too small to conceal an eight-year-old.

The top flaps of the carton in the aisle were closed but not interlocked or taped. She turned them back and found a white earthenware plate resting in an open nest of crumpled newspaper, on top of a pile of what must be matching plates wrapped in newspaper.

Someone had been interrupted while packing or unpacking a set of dinnerware.

She scrambled to her feet, scurried back to the corridor, and shouted again.

And this time, barely audible over the distant drone of the dryers, she heard an answer—a faint wail, almost a mew. It might have been the cry of a distressed kitten trying to find its way back to its littermates. It came from somewhere farther along the corridor.

Several feet beyond the storage room, the corridor ended at a blank wall, and just before that cul-de-sac, on the opposite side of the corridor from the storage room, was the door to the boiler room. From where she stood, she could see that it was closed.

Once more she ran.

The knob turned in her hand. With a surge of relief, she pushed the door open and stepped into a cavernous space crowded with the massively complex equipment designed to keep twenty stories of living space at a livable temperature.

"Melody!" she shouted.

Again she heard that little mew. It was louder this time, and now she was able to locate it. It came from far back in the depths of the boiler room. And then, back there, she heard a scuffling sound.

"Melody!" she screamed at the top of her lungs. The effort rasped her throat. *"Where are you?"*

Once more she heard the scuffling, now continuous, and then, miraculously, Melody came scrambling forward from far back behind a tangle of pipes, her hair flying, her face smudged with tears and dust. She cannoned against Martha's thighs, flung her arms around Martha's hips, and buried her face against Martha's midsection. "It's *him!*" she wailed.

Renewed scuffling in the back of the room sent a new jolt through Martha's vibrating nerves.

Peter Sanders emerged from the shadows. "Oh, thank God," he said.

"No!" Melody dug her fingers frantically into Martha's buttocks.

Peter said, "I hope she's okay. Some guy grabbed her.... Thank God you came."

Some guy?...

Melody wailed wordlessly.

"She's scared," Peter said. "Some guy grabbed her—maybe it was one of the AC people...."

"No!" Melody screamed. "It was *him!*"

Martha didn't wait. She pulled Melody's arms loose and clasped her hand, and together, hand in hand, they fled back up the corridor.

TWENTY-NINE

What Happened

TAKING A CHILD'S STATEMENT is a ticklish business, hedged around with a thicket of official rules and ad hoc precautions. Detective White and a woman whom he introduced as Detective Sylvia Rosen took Melody's statement in her own living room. She sat on a sofa between her mother and her father, who, summoned from the bowling alley, had arrived almost simultaneously with the detectives. When it became clear that the little witness was apt to pitch a tantrum if Martha wasn't allowed to stay, Martha had been allowed to stay.

Repeated assurances, by a red-faced Jeff and by both detectives, that reform school was not, had never been, and would never be in the picture, were necessary before Melody could be induced to tell them what had happened in the basement, but once she accepted the assurances, she told her story fluently.

She had been playing with her ball in the corridor outside the laundry room. *Right* outside the laundry room, she emphasized, casting an anxious glance at her mother, who cast an anxious glance across Melody's head at Jeff, who scowled but held his peace.

The ball had hit the wall "crooked" (Melody's word) and bounced away down the corridor, around the corner, and all the way to the dead end. Melody had chased after it, and on the way past the storage room, she had seen a man. "And it was him."

"Him?" queried Detective Rosen gently.

Melody squirmed to put an inch of space between herself and her father, looked at her knees, and mumbled, "The man in the stairs."

Jeff's scowl intensified.

"Tell me about the stairs," prompted Detective Rosen, still gently.

Melody tried to squirm still farther from Jeff. He laid his arm along the sofa back, clasped her shoulder, and drew her toward him. "It's okay," he said. The caress seemed to repeat the promise: *No reform school.*

Still hesitant, Melody looked across at Martha.

Hoping she had read Jeff's gesture accurately, Martha risked a cautious nod.

The dam, weakened by the previous breaches, broke once more, and again the stairwell story came pouring out. Jeff breathed in and out. Detective Rosen listened, nodding now and then. Detective White scribbled.

"And I came *straight home,*" Melody finished.

"And today?" Detective Rosen prodded gently.

"He was down in the basement, and he grabbed me."

"Can you tell me what made you think he was the same man?" asked Detective Rosen.

Melody's back stiffened. "I didn't *think* he was the same!" she declared. "It *was* him!"

"How did you know?"

"His hair was the same."

"Mm-hm?"

"It *was!* I'm telling the *truth!*"

"Don't get mad at me, okay? I'm just trying to see it the way you did. He's bigger than you. In the stairs, you saw the top of his head because he was going down and you were higher than he was. How did you see the top of his head this time?"

"He was squunched down on the floor, looking in a box." Melody slipped free of Jeff's arm, dropped to her knees on the floor, and tilted her head forward. "Like *this*. And I was over *there*...." She pointed to Detective Rosen.

"Okay, now I see."

"I saw him another time," Melody volunteered suddenly. She looked at Martha. "You were there."

Confused, Martha asked, "Do you mean outside the ice-cream store? When you and Tyler were looking down on the people coming up the subway stairs?" That hadn't been Peter Sanders; that had been Everett Upton.

But Melody shook her head. "That wasn't him. I thought it was him, but then it wasn't. He didn't have the right hair. He had funny hair. The time I mean was out in front. You were talking to Tyler's mom, and Tyler was teasing me, and I went up on that cement place around the bushes by the steps, and he came out and you talked to him, and then he went down to the sidewalk and I saw him the same way I did in the stairs. And it was him.''

"Oh, yes, I remember." Martha looked at Detective Rosen. "It was Sunday afternoon two weeks ago, the day Arnold Stern was killed."

"Did you know who he was?" asked Detective Rosen.

"Peter Sanders," Martha said. "He's the nephew of one of the residents."

"And it was him today," said Melody.

Detective Rosen looked at Martha. Martha nodded. Melody got up off the floor and clambered back onto the sofa. "He came running at me, and I tried to get away, but he grabbed me...."

Jeff stirred. "Where did he touch you?" he demanded.

"Oh." Melody looked at Vanessa. "Not there," she said. "Not that place where you said. He grabbed my arm and put his hand over my mouth, and I tried to yell, but I couldn't. And then he pushed me across the hall to that room and—" She raised her hands to encircle her neck.

Jeff's arm tightened around Melody's shoulders, and his scowl became a glower.

"I kept trying to yell." She clapped a hand over her mouth and screamed. Even muffled by her hand, the cry was not quiet; it could have penetrated the boiler room door enough to be that mewing sound Martha had heard. Melody looked across at her. "And then I heard you yell, and I tried to yell some more, and he let me go, and you came, and we ran and got Mommy, and we ran up the stairs and went out in the lobby."

Both detectives looked at Martha. She nodded.

"And he told a lie," Melody said. "He said it was somebody else but there wasn't anybody else. It was him." Her frown was so much like Jeff's that Martha nearly laughed. "People," Melody declared, "shouldn't say things they don't mean."

EPILOGUE

"SO ANSWER ME a question," said Hannah, stirring her iced tea. They had met for lunch at the crowded little cafeteria adjacent to the Whitney Museum of American Art before entering the museum to view an exhibition of contemporary quilts in which Hannah had succeeded in interesting Martha. "Why did she tell you to look at the will if it was going to tip you off that he had a motive?"

Martha didn't answer at once.

"Or aren't you supposed to talk about the will?"

"I've been talking about the will for the past ten minutes," said Martha. "It's in probate. It's a matter of public record. Confidentiality is no constraint."

"Lovely. I mean the public record part, not the probate part. I don't cheer when an old woman dies."

"She wasn't all that old. I doubt if she was any older than you."

"All the more reason she shouldn't die." Hannah laid down the spoon and sipped the tea. "He killed her, too."

"Tobacco killed her," Martha said. "Her lungs were destroyed and her heart gave out."

"He broke it."

"No, she died before she knew. She was dead before the police arrived at the hospital to interview her."

"She knew already."

"Well..." Martha applied her fork to a wedge of quiche. "I suppose she could have. In that dreadful way that one knows and resolves not to."

Hannah answered her own question: "She knew, and she couldn't let him get away with it, but she couldn't bring herself to set the dogs on him. So she set you up to do it by shoving the will in front of your nose."

"You may be right," said Martha. "There's another question that bothers me more. Since she was making him the contingent residuary legatee, why did she put in that insulting five-dollar bequest and all that angry language?"

"She had to scold him, but she felt bad."

Martha shook her head. "It doesn't make sense."

"Sense, schmense. He made her mad with the name thing, so she shoved the will at him to show him what it would cost him. But he didn't change his name back, he killed her dear friend instead, and then she realized she'd set him up, and that killed her."

"I wonder if she was that complex."

"Sure she was. It was a family thing, the name change and the money all tangled up together. You think families are simple?"

"No. And she did have a grim view of the institution. She once suggested that all married people want to kill each other."

"They don't?"

"Hannah, don't start."

"Eight years old." The assistant district attorney shook his head. He was a senior ADA who had been around many blocks many times; Martha took his head-shaking seriously.

She had been called to his office to tell him everything she knew about Melody's stairwell adventure, and everything she had seen and heard in the basement. The stairwell story, of course, was inadmissible hearsay, consisting as it did of a secondhand account of something Melody had said, but it was useful for filling in the prosecutor's grasp of the events. Martha's part in the basement events, however, was within her personal experience, so her testimony would be admissible when Peter was charged with kidnapping and unlawful imprisonment.

The ADA shook his head again. "Eight years old. Competency problems right up front, and her father being questioned as a suspect puts her credibility in question."

"She's a tough-minded little girl," said Martha. "She knows what she knows. I wouldn't want the job of cross-examining her."

"Nobody wants to cross-examine a kid. Nobody wants to deal with a kid's testimony, period." He shuffled papers without looking at them. "Well, we may be able to get by without her stairwell story. He admits he was up there."

"At Arnold's?"

"He went up to ask Stern's advice about getting his dear old auntie a gun for self-defense."

"He says." Martha let skepticism color her tone.

"No witnesses to say different. Old lady living alone, lax security, doormen changing all the time; he could have wanted her to have a gun."

"That's an exaggeration," Martha protested. "The building has had one new doorman in the past six years."

"Then I expect he'll be advised to drop the doorman. There's still the lone old lady."

"How does he explain firing Arnold's gun into Arnold's face?"

"Accident."

"They didn't know it was loaded?" Once more sarcasm charged Martha's voice.

"He didn't fill in the blanks. It was right about then that he decided he'd better exercise his Miranda rights."

Martha said, "I'd expect someone who'd been involved in a fatal gun accident to call 911 right away, not go running down the stairs and out of the building with a bag of clothes for his dear old auntie in the ICU."

The ADA didn't react. That, Martha supposed, was going to be a prosecution argument.

"How does he explain his attack on Melody?" she persisted. "The only plausible motive is that he'd shot Arnold deliberately and he knew she'd seen him in the stairs."

"He didn't attack her."

"Oh, please."

This time the ADA let himself smile a bit. "He claims."

"That's absurd."

"Yes, it is. Everybody on the air-conditioning crew had left, and for a wonder, they're all alibied six ways to Sunday. The police searched the place and found no evidence of anyone else in the basement. If little Miss Melody holds up under cross, and if you hang in there, the abduction charges—knock wood—are in decent shape."

"But the homicide is all circumstantial," she said.

He shrugged without speaking.

"I suppose her testimony about seeing him leaving the scene of the homicide would establish a motive for the abduction."

"Establishing motive isn't necessary, but it never hurts." He shuffled papers again, and this time he looked at one of them. "You made a statement about that Greek pot that turned up in the victim's apartment. About Everett Upton's having handled it. Do you have anything to add to it?"

"Is it going to be an issue?" she asked.

"Not if I can help it. The old auntie said she gave it to the victim to keep safe for her and nobody's saying any different. You confirm that Everett Upton handled it in your presence, and they haven't found any unexplained fingerprints on it, so we don't have any reason to complicate the case by opening it up. The Met is making a pitch to get the thing released to the estate so they can get their grubby mitts on it." He stood up and held out his hand. "Thanks for coming. Somebody will call you."

No unexplained fingerprints on the kylix meant that Fiona's weren't on it, which meant that Fiona's tale of stealing it was false.

Which left Everett as the thief.

Briefly, Martha asked herself if she should have told someone about Fiona's flimsy yarn. Her answer was no. The kylix's wanderings didn't matter. The crime was homicide, not theft. The police had the right man, and the kylix would ultimately arrive at its intended destination.

The answering machine was blinking when she got home. She pressed play. Helen Taubensee's mature female voice said, "I'm calling to clear up that thing Mackie told us about. Would you call me back, please?"

Martha called her back.

Mackie McGarrity knew only part of the story, said Helen Taubensee. "I thought I'd better speak to the person in question. She showed me receipts. As far as I can tell, she paid full price for the items."

"That's good," said Martha. Receipts could be forged, but the problem wasn't hers.

"Have you made any sense out of that anonymous phone call she says she got?" asked Helen.

"I think Peter must have made it," said Martha. "I think you were on the right track. It seems to me it had to be a harebrained attempt by whoever killed Arnold to try to cast suspicion on aggrieved shareholders.''

''Messing up people's lives?''

''Just so.''

''Did he hear the girls say that?''

''I'm afraid he heard it from me, when I was telling Irene about the shareholders' revolt and the controversy over the nursery.''

''What a shame about Irene.''

''Very much so.''

''Well, that's all very gruesome and interesting, but it isn't really what I called about. What I called about is to ask if you are still interested in serving on the board. Because if you are, we'd like to interview you before the next meeting.''

Oh, dear. Was she interested?

She knew the conspirators had been lobbying the board to appoint her, and she hadn't directed them to stop lobbying, so maybe she was interested. No, *maybe* was too feeble. Faced with the ultimate yes versus no, she admitted what she had been trying to deny. She had a promise to keep—she must do what she could to repeal the dog rule.

''Yes, I am,'' she said.

''Oh, excellent. And will you support me in passing a house rule barring homicidal nephews from visiting their aunts?''

Working with this woman should be entertaining. ''It's a thought,'' Martha said, ''but wouldn't it be simpler just to ban guns?''

AN ELDERHOSTEL MYSTERY
PAINTED LADY
PETER ABRESCH

James P. Dandy and his ladylove, Dodee Swisher, embark on an Elderhostel adventure along the old Santa Fe Trail. But before the trip even gets under way, Jim sees a Native American woman plunge to her death from a Denver rooftop. He suspects that the woman was pushed.

Soon it's clear somebody thinks Jim knows the whereabouts of a priceless Mayan artifact—a misconception that is becoming dangerous to both Jim and Dodee.

Another grisly murder occurs on the historic trail through the Wild West, and mysteries old and new find Jim caught in a shoot-out with a killer determined to make this Dandy's Last Stand.

"…a suspect-rich plot with a revealing glimpse of small-town life… evocative descriptions of the desert and mountains of the Southwest."
—*Booklist*

Available April 2004 at your favorite retail outlet.

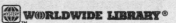 **W⊙RLDWIDE LIBRARY**®

WPA488

DOROTHY KLIEWER

MURDER
IN THE SWAMP
A DEEDRA MASEFIELD MYSTERY

A woman's body is dragged from the fetid, swampy end of a
tiny lake. She is the latest victim in a string of murders, and
newspaper reporter Deedra Masefield is determined to break
the story. None of the longtime residents of this desolate
California town is above suspicion.

Barely surviving a plunge into the frigid, terrifying depths of
the swamp herself, Deedra discovers grisly secrets beneath
the surface and makes the stunning connection between the
murderer and his victims. She's finally got her killer story—
she's just got to live long enough to tell it.

Available April 2004 at your favorite retail outlet.

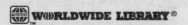

WDK490

DESPERATE JOURNEYS

Four trips you *won't* want to take...

DESERT DECEIT by Betty Webb
The murder of a media magnate turns a dude-ranch cattle drive into a trail full of unforeseen danger. Vacationing private eye Lena Jones attempts to unmask a killer in Arizona's most rugged and remote area.

THE FIRST PROOF by Terence Faherty
Ex-seminarian Owen Keane accompanies his former lover to Maine to bury her estranged husband. But dark mysteries surrounding the dead man's family converge as a murderer strikes at the heart of a tragic past filled with buried secrets, blackmail and vengeance.

DEATH ON THE SOUTHWEST CHIEF by Jonathan Harrington
Danny O'Flaherty escorts his eccentric aunt on a cross-country train trip, only to discover his uncle's corpse in the next seat. When the body is stolen and replaced with that of a freshly strangled man, Danny has seventy-two hours to find a killer.

STAR SEARCH by Nancy Baker Jacobs
Hollywood Star reporter Quinn Collins inherits a house from a writer she never knew. Looking into blacklisted writers of the 1950s proves dangerous as Quinn exposes a killer's desperate scheme—and the stunning truth about her own parents.

Available May 2004 at your favorite retail outlet.

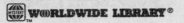

WDJ491